Alinta Lawrence is helping her partner establish a sheep station (what the Australians call a ranch) in her native Outback but learning the white man's ways is a challenge for the primitive woman. While raising a child with Mel, she is amazed and sometimes overwhelmed by the many "things" these white people seem to need in their lives. Will she be able to cope with all the changes life presents and keep their family together?

A K'Anne Meinel novella

Novels in Paperback:

SHIPS *CompanionSHIP, FriendSHIP, RelationSHIP*
Long Distance Romance
Children of Another Mother
Erotica
The Claim
Bikini's Are Dangerous
The Complete Series
Germanic
Malice Masterpieces 1
The First Five Books
Represented
Timed Romance
Malice Masterpieces 2
Books Six through Ten
The Journey Home
Out at the Inn
Shorts
Anthology Volume 1
Lawyered
Malice Masterpieces 3
Books Eleven through Fifteen
Blown Away

Blown Away
The Alternate Cover
Small Town Angel
Pirated Love
Doctored
Veil of Silence
Malice Masterpieces 4
Books Sixteen through Twenty
The Outsider
Pirated Heart
Recombinant Love
Survivors
Inn the Dog House
Flight
An Island Between Us

Vetted Series:
Vetted
Cavalcade (Prequel)
Pioneering (Prequel)
Vetted Further
Vetted Again

Novellas in Paperback:

Mysterious Malice (Book 1)
Meticulous Malice (Book 2)
Mistaken Malice (Book 3)
Malicious Malice (Book 4)
Masterful Malice (Book 5)
Matrimonial Malice (Book 6)
Mourning Malice (Book 7)
Murderous Malice (Book 8)
Mental Malice (Book 9)
Menacing Malice (Book 10)
Minor Malice (Book 11)
Morally Malice (Book 12)
Morose Malice (Book 13)
Melancholy Malice (Book 14)
Mad Malice (Book 15)
Macabre Malice (Book 16)
Marinating Malice (Book 17)

Macerating Malice (Book 18)
Minacious Malice (Book 19)
Meddlesome Malice (Book 20)
Meandering Malice (Book 21)
Vaquera Safica (Spanish)
Surfista Safica (Spanish)
ケーアンヌ・マイネル (Japanese)
Maniacal Malice (Book 22)
Sayyida
The Northwood Lodge
Monitoring Malice (Book 23)
Marked Malice (Book 24)
Shanghaied
Outback Born
Outback Bred
Outback Heritage

Pocket Paperbacks:

Mysterious Malice (Book 1)
Sapphic Surfer
Sapphic Cowgirl
Meticulous Malice (Book 2)
Mistaken Malice (Book 3)
Malicious Malice (Book 4)
Masterful Malice (Book 5)
Matrimonial Malice (Book 6)
Mourning Malice (Book 7)
Murderous Malice (Book 8)

Mental Malice (Book 9)
Menacing Malice (Book 10)
Minor Malice (Book 11)
Morally Malice (Book 12)
Morose Malice (Book 13)
Melancholy Malice (Book 14)
Mad Malice (Book 15)
Macabre Malice (Book 16)
Marinating Malice (Book 17)

In E-Book Format:
Short Stories

Fantasy
Wet & Wet Again
Family Night
Quickie ~ Against the Car
Quickie ~ Against the Wall
Quickie ~ Over the Couch
Mile High Club
Quickie ~ Under the Pier
Heel or Heal
Kiss
Family Night 2
Beach Dreams
Internet Dreamers
Snoggered

On the Parkway
Stable Affair
Kept
Stolen
Agitated
Love of my LIFE
Quickie in an Elevator,
GOING DOWN?
Into the Garden
The Book Case
The Other Women
Menage a WHAT?

E-Book Novellas

Children of Another Mother
Bikini's are Dangerous
Ghostly Love
Bikini's are Dangerous 2
Sapphic Surfer
The Rockhound
Bikini's are Dangerous 3
Bikini's are Dangerous 4
Bikini's are Dangerous 5
Mysterious Malice (Book 1)
Meticulous Malice (Book 2)
Mistaken Malice (Book 3)
Malicious Malice (Book 4)
Masterful Malice (Book 5)
Matrimonial Malice (Book 6)
Mourning Malice (Book 7)
Murderous Malice (Book 8)
Sapphic Cowgirl
Sapphic Cowboi
Mental Malice (Book 9)
Menacing Malice (Book 10)
Charming Thief
~Snake Island~

Charming Thief
~Diamonds are a Girls Best Friend~
Minor Malice (Book 11)
Morally Malice (Book 12)
Morose Malice (Book 13)
Melancholy Malice (Book 14)
Mad Malice (Book 15)
Macabre Malice (Book 16)
Marinating Malice (Book 17)
Macerating Malice (Book 18)
Minacious Malice (Book 19)
Sayyida
Meddlesome Malice (Book 20)
Meandering Malice (Book 21)
Maniacal Malice (Book 22)
The Northwood Lodge
Monitoring Malice (Book 23)
Marked Malice (Book 24)
Shanghaied
Outback Born
Outback Bred
Outback Heritage

E-Book Novels

SHIPS *CompanionSHIP, FriendSHIP, RelationSHIP*
Erotica Volume 1
Long Distance Romance
Bikini's Are Dangerous
The Complete Series
Malice Masterpieces
The First Five Books
To Love a Shooting Star
Germanic
The Claim
Represented
Timed Romance
Blown Away
Blown Away *The Alternate Cover*
Malice Masterpieces 2
Books Six through Ten
The Journey Home
Out at the Inn
Anthology Volume 1
Lawyered

Malice Masterpieces 3
Books Eleven through Fifteen
Small Town Angel
Pirated Love
Doctored
Veil of Silence
Malice Masterpieces 4
Books Sixteen through Twenty
The Outsider
Pirated Heart
Recombinant Love
Survivors
Inn the Dog House
Flight
An Island Between Us

Vetted Series:
Vetted
Cavalcade (Prequel)
Pioneering (Prequel)
Vetted Further
Vetted Again

LARGE Print Novels

SHIPS CompanionSHIP, FriendSHIP, RelationSHIP
Erotica Volume 1
Long Distance Romance
Children of Another Mother
Bikini's Are Dangerous
The Complete Series

Malice Masterpieces
The First Five Books
To Love a Shooting Star
The Claim
Represented
Timed Romance

Audiobooks

Doctored
Sapphic Surfer
The Rockhound
Cavalcade

Pioneering
To Love A Shooting Star
Mysterious Malice

Videos

Biography of Books
Ships
Sapphic Surfer
Ghostly Love
Long Distance Romance
Germanic
Sensual Sapphic
Sapphic Cowgirl
Couples
Lie Next To Me

Sapphic Cowboi
Timed Romance
Readings (SHIPS)
Doctored
Veil of Silence
She's Coming (The Outsider short)
It's Coming (The Outsider short)
The Outsider
Vetted

K'ANNE MEINEL

OUTBACK

NATIVE

ISBN-13: 978-1733661188

K'Anne Meinel is available for comments at KAnneMeinel@aim.com as well as on Facebook @ http://www.facebook.com/K.Anne.Meinel.Fan.Page, Google + @ https://plus.google.com/u/2/+KAnneMeinel, LinkedIn @ https://www.linkedin.com/in/k-anne-meinel-a026385a, or her blog @ http://kannemeinel.wordpress.com/ or on Twitter @ https://twitter.com/KAnneMeinel, or on her website @ www.kannemeinel.com if you would like to follow her to find out about stories and book's releases.

www.shadoepublishing.com

ShadoePublishing@gmail.com

Shadoe Publishing, LLC is a United States of America company

Cover by: K'Anne Meinel @ Shadoe Publishing
Edited by: Deb Amia, Grammar Queen grammarqueen.com

**Dedicated to anyone who
thinks I'm writing about them.
I am.**

CHAPTER ONE

Alinta looked down the long line of carts filled with supplies that followed them and beyond them to the huge flock of sheep her husband owned. She didn't yet understand the concept of ownership, so she always thought of everything as Mel's property only. She watched the dingo-like dogs on both sides of the flock and the new men, who were helping to herd over ten thousand sheep. Clouds of dust were churned up by the tens of thousands of hooves, and it filtered over the land of the Outback. When they stopped, it also settled over the people, the horses, and the sheep themselves. Alinta looked to her husband riding beside her and smiled. Mel had suggested that she ride astride since it would be easier to maintain her balance than with the sidesaddle she had previously ridden. She was finding that gripping the sides of the horse was much easier than maintaining her balance on top of a

sidesaddle. She was holding their small, one-month-old daughter in a clever wrap she had contrived, which would hold the infant and keep her safe as she rode. It also allowed her to breastfeed the little girl when she became hungry and freed her arms to hold the reins of the horse as she rode. She was learning to really like these strange beasts she hadn't known in her life while growing up. She found them to be intelligent, mostly kind, and very helpful. She could still use her own legs to travel, but they seemed to go much farther and much faster when on the animals. Now, with their daughter Ainia to carry, she was appreciative of the animals' strength.

Alinta saw the domed hills up ahead and was pleased. It meant they would soon be on the land her husband had claimed for the station she was establishing. Alinta understood now that these white people needed ownership of the land, and while she didn't understand all the subtleties of it yet, she was learning. Mel had called it Lawrence Station, signifying by using her name that she had ownership of the land. Alinta too claimed part of Mel's name as her own now. She was known as Alinta Lawrence, and she liked that. It meant she belonged to Mel for always. Mel had explained that since they were now married, they belonged to each other for always. Alinta took comfort in that fact.

The long line of carts slowed as men dismounted and began clearing a path using the various tools they called machetes, axes, and shovels. The tools allowed them to make what they called a track into Lawrence Station, which joined up with the station they had just left that was owned by their friends, Fabiola and Carmen. It was called Twin Station. Alinta had never had friends before and was pleased that she was learning to appreciate these women, who called themselves her friends too. Alinta saw the men were making the track towards the first of the folds she and Mel had built when they came to this virgin land with their flock the previous year. At that time, there had been only four thousand sheep, but Mel had chosen mature, three- and four-year-old sheep, so they would have twins and even higher multiples when they began birthing. The sheep had exceeded her expectations, and now, they had over ten thousand sheep. Alinta didn't comprehend numbers that high, but Mel had taught her to count in English on her fingers and was now teaching her how she could learn the concept of even higher numbers by using her own fingers and toes and the idea of other people's hands. She delighted in this learning and was eager to know as much as Mel. The white woman knew so much because she had been to school and had tutors, and she took delight in helping Alinta learn these things.

Mel had explained that they would leave some of the sheep at a fold with one of the men and possibly a younger man or boy called a jackaroo or assistant. Alinta didn't understand exactly what a jackaroo did, but she knew it was to help with the sheep, and that was good enough for her.

Mel had also explained that they would be building this track to connect the different folds until they arrived where she wanted to build their home station. From there, another track would go out from their station to other tracks that would lead to towns. Alinta remembered towns from the time of her capture and didn't like the idea of ever going back to one. It had been fascinating to visit a store, but she didn't understand most of the things she saw there. Now, many of those things were carried in their supplies, and Mel had ordered many more to use in establishing the station she so badly wanted. Alinta could sense Mel's enthusiasm for it, and while she didn't fully understand the concept, she wanted desperately to help her husband in any way she could. Mel was so patient about explaining these things to the aboriginal woman, who couldn't relate these ideas to anything in her own culture. Now that she was in the white man's world, she would accept these things because Mel explained them to her.

The tracks that flowed east and south from their station led towards other more established tracks that eventually connected to towns and would enable them to receive the many more sheep and other supplies Mel had ordered to be brought to their station. In the meantime, Mel still had to build the tracks, the folds to hold the sheep, and their home. Home for Alinta was wherever Mel was, and she was content with that. She didn't need a house, something she now understood from their two visits to Twin Station where they stayed in one of the extra stockmen's houses. Mel promised to build her a house when they eventually got the track built to where she wanted their home. Alinta understood the house would stand next to that beautiful, lush, green valley Mel had found. It was full of long grasses, a stream meandered through it, and there was even a waterfall. It was a very pleasant place, and Alinta had loved it almost as much as Mel.

Alinta musingly wondered when the kissing that she and Mel had done previously would start up again. She also knew there was more, but she didn't know what. She just knew she yearned for more than they had. Mel was now her mate for all time according to the man with the book, who had married them and baptized their daughter, Ainia, pronounced ah-nee-ah. Mel had assured her that the baptism was a Christian thing, and she was grateful to know that her daughter was saved. She wasn't sure what she was saved from, but Mel seemed pleased that they were legally married, and their daughter was saved for eternity. One of the men addressed Alinta, and she was pleased when they referred to her as Mrs. Lawrence. Mel had explained this was a sign of respect since they were now married. Having two names wasn't exactly new to Alinta since she had had her tribal affiliation previously, but she had never found the need to use it before. Her family and her tribe had known she belonged, but the white people had a completely different concept, and she was trying to learn it and understand it. She looked at Ainia again and smiled. Her daughter had three names, Ainia Mary Lawrence, and she was named after an Amazon woman. Amazons were a different tribe of warrior women, and Alinta was proud of the name Mel had chosen for their daughter. Her daughter would be raised as a white woman, and as the aboriginal woman looked at the infant, she could already see her daughter looked whiter than any baby born to her tribe. She was proud of her daughter.

A second fire was made for the men who worked for Mel, this one nearer the fold and the sheep. Alinta would have made enough food for all of them, but Mel had stopped her. Mel explained she was only to make enough food for herself, Mel, and Ainia plus any special guests. She explained that the men, including those two with wives, would remain separate because that was how it was done. Mel had further explained that these were employees that worked for them. Alinta didn't completely understand about employees, but the new women, the wives of the men, had been kind to her, and she appreciated that.

Mel fed the dogs that evening, praising them, talking to them, and petting them. She gave a little extra to the two bitches who had given birth since their pups were still young and nursing. Alinta liked carrying those pups in bags attached to her saddle. They were so cute

and small. Their anxious mothers followed her horse closely and were eager anytime she stopped for them to feed their offspring. She understood how they felt as she held Ainia closer. She prepared rice, peas, and mutton for their family, and as a bonus, she had added some natural fruits she found that seemed to grow all over. She knew Mel appreciated these, and she knew Mel was relieved when she had stopped eating grubs and other insects as well as snakes and rodents. Mel hadn't ordered her to stop, but she had seen the faces Mel made when she ate them, and she learned that Mel found them repugnant.

That night, they snuggled together in the hastily built hut and kissed, but Mel stopped them before things went any further. Alinta would acquiesce to anything Mel wanted, trusting her and allowing her to take the lead since she knew nothing of what was to come. Sometime during the night, Ainia started fussing, and Alinta rose to change the baby, shushing her with crooning sounds and feeding her, so she wouldn't wake Mel or any others. She was subliminally aware of Mel watching her as she walked and rocked the baby after feeding, and she wondered what Mel was thinking.

The next day, the men were up early harnessing the bullocks that they were using with the many carts that carried their supplies for the station. They continued cutting brush and trees, using open fields whenever possible as they cut the track into the wilderness.

CHAPTER TWO

Several weeks later, they arrived at what would be their home station. They no longer had any sheep to attend to after leaving the last of the flock with a stockman in the fifth fold Mel and Alinta had built earlier. The men that remained began to fell trees and gird them. Girding was a new term to Alinta, but Mel explained that if they cut into the trees, they would die and strengthen, and they would only fell the trees when they really needed them. Apparently, they needed a supply of wood for the house, barns, and sheds they would build. Having just come from Twin Station, Alinta now understood what those buildings would be used for.

She watched as Mel and some men unrolled string to various lengths and pounded stakes into the ground. These were the outlines of where their buildings would go.

The first building was called a bunkhouse or barracks for the men. That was another one of those dual words that confused the Aborigine because some words were American English and some were Australian English. Mel used both and laughed at herself about it. She regretted confusing Alinta but knew she would need to know both terms as she learned to speak the language and came to understand what the words meant.

Alinta was amazed as she watched the men roll rocks and boulders along these strings and cut the trees down. They cut the trees again in what they called sawpits, making the wood conform to what they wanted to build. She was astounded when they used the white man's stone—metal, she mentally corrected herself—to keep the wood in place where they desired it. She watched in awe as the building rose before her. Mel said she wanted the bunkhouse to be big enough to sleep at least two dozen men. Alinta learned that one dozen was both hands plus two toes. Two dozen meant both her hands and both Mel's hands and four toes. She found it easy to envision that in her head, and she wasn't even aware when she no longer needed to count on her fingers and toes.

Alinta learned they had to dig a pit to cut the wood. They used something called a whipsaw, one of their fantastic metal tools with teeth on its sharpened edges to dig into the trees. One of the people could saw down in this pit, but it went faster if someone was at the other end to help pull and push. Mel took a turn, and the dust drove her crazy when it settled in her shirt, wraps, and hair. Alinta went with her as she crept into the beautiful valley to bathe and rid herself of these tiny bits of wood that caused her to itch due to all the sweating she was doing in the hot sun while they sawed the trees into the required lengths of wood.

Alinta was startled when two of the men got into a confrontation about working in the saw pit. "It's your turn!" one of the stockmen told another, demanding that he go down in the pit and use the saws. The boards were building up, and the barracks was nearly complete. Mel wanted the roof made of slate, and one of the men knew how to install that using whatever flat rocks could be found. It became a game for the men to hunt for and find the flat rocks. The rocks were drilled through on one end and then nails were bored through into the wood roof, further protecting the building from the elements. Alinta enjoyed hunting for these rocks along with the other women. She would help them by using her gathering stick to pry the rocks loose from the ground or outcroppings. As always, Ainia was carried in a wrap strapped to her chest while she worked, so she could feed her when it became necessary.

"I ain't going to do it. I can't stand the dust up my nose, and my eyes itched for three days last time. I'll herd sheep, I'll cut down trees, and I'll build, but I won't go in that saw pit, and you can't make me!" the man protested.

"I'll make you!" the other man started, leaning towards the man with his fists clenched, but Mel was there by that time, having heard the ruction. Alinta stared, frightened at the raised voices and considering running away. She calmed once she saw Mel; her husband always seemed to know just what to do.

"You agreed to work for me. That means you will do *any* jobs assigned to you on this place. If you won't do your fair share, then you *won't* work for me," she told him, getting between him and the other stockman.

"You don't own all this," he gestured to the raw land around them, the piles of trees, the wood boards building up, the building they were working on, and the fences taking shape. Two of the men were marking out additional buildings that Mel wanted for a shearing shed, a couple barns, and even a chicken coop. "You just came out here and claimed all this. Who are you to order me about?" he asked belligerently.

"I thought I was your employer. You agreed to the conditions I laid out to everyone. You don't like it, then make your way back to Wilcannia."

"You'd put me off like that? After all the work I did helping you get here?"

"You agreed to work for me. I told you all it was new, it was raw, and there would be plenty of work, but I also promised you plenty of food, and you agreed. If you're not willing to do all the work, then you aren't staying on my land." She leaned in, and Alinta worried for her. She wondered what the man would do. Mel was daring him to take a swing at her, and she knew it would hurt because he was just big as she. Mel watched every move he made, hoping to duck in time when he finally made his move.

"What about my pay?" he asked, sounding angrier than Mel had guessed he could be. Alinta had seen this thing they called pay. It was little papers and metal coins that she didn't understand, but Mel had explained these things had value and were given in exchange for the work they did. Alinta didn't see how these little things could possibly be the same value as the hard work these men did, but she accepted Mel's explanation.

"I've got your pay, and I'll give you supplies for two weeks, enough to get you back to Wilcannia."

"You'd turn me into a swagman? There's other jobs I could do besides that," he gestured at the saw pit where the men were staring up, aghast at the way he was speaking to the owner.

"You're turning yourself into a swagman. You agreed to work, and you aren't doing your fair share. Gather your gear, and I'll have your supplies and pay ready." Alinta knew a swagman was a traveler, who went from station to station. Sometimes they helped with little tasks or even fighting fires while earning enough for food and supplies. Other times, they just traveled from station to station, basically asking for a handout. She'd been surprised how many people did this, having met a few of them on Twin Station, and it seemed as though they were always men. She didn't think it was much different than a walkabout, something Mel didn't understand when she tried to explain.

The man turned away, disgusted, but not before mumbling, "I'd rather not work for a coon lover anyway."

"What did you say?" Mel roared. Alinta was shocked to hear her husband's voice raised to this degree. She'd never heard the big woman shout like this before.

He turned back, finally finding the fight he had been looking for. "I said, I wouldn't want to work for a *coon lover*," he gestured towards Alinta. Alinta blinked, realizing she was being pulled into the fight and not sure what the words meant. She didn't understand, but she could see how the words were affecting Mel...she was furious!

Mel didn't hesitate. Her fist immediately came up as her father had shown her so long ago and she had so rarely used. She struck the man in his big mouth. She'd made sure her thumb was tucked in, so it wouldn't get broken. Girls tended to forget this and often broke their thumbs, but Mel hadn't been a girl in a long time. It felt good when her punch struck home, and she followed it with a left to the gut of the man, which was sticking out as his back arched from the blow to his mouth. As he bent over to take the blow to his stomach, her knee was lifting, and his head was thrown back when the bone hit his nose. He went down. Mel wiped the back of her hand across her mouth. She was breathing hard, and Alinta was tempted to go to her. "You get off my station!" she said to the downed man, "And take that as a warning," she glanced around at the other men staring in shock at the fight and the man's insubordination. "My wife is not to be disparaged in any way. I ever hear you say anything like that again," she said, looking down at the man glaring up at her belligerently, "and I'll kill you." Alinta was proud that Mel was defending her but against what she didn't know. At the same time, several people glanced at her, and she was frightened over the fight. She hadn't known two people could get so violent. Her people had never done things like that. She'd heard of them fighting to steal women, but that was done in stealth and was rarely physical.

The man looked up fearfully now. Everything had happened so quickly that he hadn't been prepared. He was tempted to continue the fight, but the look in Mel's dark brown eyes told him this man *would* kill him. Had he known he was really facing a woman; he would have been so humiliated he would have been forced to fight back. He nodded, one hard nod as he looked away and gingerly felt his jaw and broken nose.

"Half an hour. Roll your swag. I'll have your pay ready, and you get out of here," Mel told him with finality, looking up at the staring men. "Get back to work. Any of you feel the same way he does, come see me, and I'll have your pay ready and give you enough supplies to get back to Wilcannia." Mel turned to go where the supplies were stacked neatly under a tarp and began measuring out what she had promised the man.

"I will be going with me mate," a voice behind Mel said tentatively as she measured. She glanced up to see who it was, nodded once, and doubled the portions she was pouring into bags. By the time she was done, the two men had gathered their rolls, their hats, and their coats, and she handed them the bag of supplies and their pay. She watched as they began to make their way to the southeast, towards where the men had begun cutting a trail through the trees and brush and where she would eventually cut a track to be connected to civilization.

Mel washed her knuckles in a cold bucket of water, shaking now that the men were gone, and the confrontation was over. Alinta watched her carefully, having never witnessed such violence between two human beings. She had seen what had happened when she was captured but had thought that merely an isolated incident. It frightened her, and she hadn't understood all the words.

Dinner that night was rather quiet and not only around their fire. Everyone went to bed early.

That night as they lay in their hut, Alinta asked, "What is coon lover?"

Mel could feel the anger and disgust she had felt that afternoon building up again. "You don't need–" she began but realized that wasn't fair to her wife. Alinta didn't know how cruel the white man

could be, and then she rethought that as Ainia began suckling. Alinta did indeed know how cruel the white man could be, and this child was the result of that rape. "He was referring to the color of your skin. Some men think having darker skin means you are less human than they are. The word coon refers to someone with darker skin, and it is not a kind word."

Alinta didn't know if she should be upset but thought perhaps Mel had taken care of it for her. She didn't understand all the implications of the word. "There are those with darker skin than mine," she commented.

"I think I have the prettiest wife," Mel murmured, laying on her side, smiling and watching as Alinta fed Ainia.

"Pretty is like flower?" Alinta asked, trying to be sure of the meaning of the word. Mel had picked her flowers one day, but she had misunderstood and thought they were to eat. She shredded them but found no food value in the flowers, and Mel had explained why someone would give another such things.

"Or like a sunrise or sunset," Mel explained, pleased to get off the subject of the men and their foul mouths. She felt very protective of her wife and child, and she wouldn't let anyone disparage them in any way.

CHAPTER THREE

Mel sent some of the men ahead to begin building the track towards where there was another track that it was rumored would connect them with civilization. The men who stayed continued to work on the home station. Already, a basement, or a cellar had been dug for the main house. Lined with rocks, a sturdy foundation rose above the grounds. Big heavy trees had been rolled onto these foundations and boards were placed across them for the first floor. Alinta didn't understand the building but found it fascinating to see what these white people created. She had no concept of floors or basements and was simply marveling at what they had invented.

Alinta didn't like it when Mel went with some of the men to help build the track towards the one remaining fold the two of them had built together. She watched as a couple men took supplies to the men

who remained at the other folds in charge of their sheep. Mel and several of the men had blocked up the creek that flowed across the track they had already built and the new one they were making. This formed a pond, and the women helped Alinta make a garden, explaining how they could grow their own fruits and vegetables, and they would use the water from the pond to keep the plants alive in the hot, Australian sun. Alinta realized how useful this would be. She wouldn't have to hunt and scavenge for fruits and vegetables any longer, so she helped with the garden. She was eager to learn all she could from these ladies. One of the men knew how to build a water wheel, which would help the water flow up to the garden and keep their plants wet. Alinta found this all very fascinating and realized that these people made convenient things that her own people would never have thought of.

Alinta helped wherever she could as she got to know the women better. She was quiet and observant, rarely asking questions even when she didn't understand the things they did. Once she was shown what to do though, she was eager to help and cheerfully kept at it. The women were cautiously friendly to the aboriginal woman, aware that she was the wife of the owner. Alinta wasn't aware of their hesitancy as she helped dig in the garden and learned the difference between a weed and the plants they were cultivating. She also helped to plant other seeds that Mel had shipped in. She learned new words and names for plants that weren't familiar to her, and she helped extensively in this amazing idea…a garden. The women were kind to the native woman and taught her, keenly aware that she had the ear of the owner and not certain she wouldn't complain to Mel if they were unkind to her. After all, their

husbands' livelihoods depended on this station, and so far, Mel had been a good employer.

Ainia hung in the wrap Alinta had made, never far from her mother's heartbeat as the woman worked. The other women, one who had a young son of her own, cooed over the baby. For the first time, Alinta felt as though she belonged, and it was an odd feeling. The women remained respectful and shared things with her, although they might not have shared everything they would have shared with their contemporaries. They exclaimed over their little community and explored the immediate vicinity around the home paddocks.

One of the men returned from taking supplies out to the stockmen. He was leading the stockman's horse with the stockman sitting on it. The stockman's leg was a pulpy mess after being gored by a wild boar. Another stockman saw this and immediately drew supplies and set out to cover the fold where they had left the sheep with only a jackaroo to tend the flock. Alinta got to work on the injured man. She used wild plants she had gathered to cleanse the wound, spiderwebs to stop the bleeding, and a sewing needle that Mel had given her to practice sewing clothing to sew the wound shut. She made the man get up and walk on it at least twice a day as it healed, and he didn't like her for that. The other men warned him not to say anything, telling of the fight and the subsequent firing of the man who had left, but he already knew the story. Those who brought him supplies had left out nothing in the telling, so he was careful what he said to the aboriginal woman, despite her constantly nagging him to walk. She tried to explain he would heal faster if he was up and about, and she had found him a forked branch to hobble around on. He knew he was lucky to be alive. Wild boars are vicious, and this one would have killed him if the dogs hadn't

distracted the animal and allowed him to get off a shot that hit behind the ear of the beast.

Alinta was pleased to see Mel return after her many weeks away. She and some of the men returned dragging trees down the new track they were building and adding them to the large pile at the home station that the other men had been sawing up. She sent additional men back down the track to fetch even more of the logs they had cut. Alinta told her of the man who had been gored by the wild boar, and Mel went to see him immediately.

"How are you doing?" she asked him.

"Fair to middling. Your missus has been looking after me."

"I heard," Mel said, amused and waiting for the man to say something. She was hoping he wasn't too angry based on what the other stockmen and her wife had told her.

"You know, she's a bit of nag," he began and saw Mel stiffen, "but she was right. It's healin' fair to dinkum fast." He grinned to show he didn't hold any ill will towards Alinta and had been teasing to lessen the pain he was feeling.

Mel grinned, nodding. "She'll have you in good shape in no time."

"Will I get my place back?" he fretted.

"You want to go back?"

"Aye, I kind of like the place, and if you'll help me write a letter, I'd like to send for my missus to come with the supply train."

"I'll do that," Mel promised. Now that the track was nearly open to Wilcannia, they could send a rider there periodically for the mail. Some men needed to blow off steam sometimes, and she was certain someone would be willing to go when she was ready to send off more correspondence.

Alinta resumed working in the garden, and Mel went down into the hidden valley to work on fences. Alinta was the first to see the large dust cloud coming from the new track to the southeast several months later. She understood the concept of direction now. Mel had explained that the sun came up in the east and set in the west, and she showed Alinta where north and south were. She had also explained that directions helped to show people where to go. Alinta shaded her eyes as others noticed the dust cloud too. One man came running up the track from where he had been working, his horse dragging trees. He tied the horse to one of the fences and yelled.

"Where is Mr. Mel?" Alinta and several others pointed towards the well-worn path leading to the hidden valley. He ran on foot to wave her down.

A while later, Mel rode up the path, and the man explained there were cattle and other animals coming down the track. Others gathered around to hear his news, and Mel could now see the dust cloud. She looked up at the clouds, and Alinta knew this meant she was concerned about the weather. It was almost time for the rains to come, and they'd already gotten a few small squalls.

"Have a few men ready to help when they get past the creek," Mel ordered, and the man ran off to comply.

Alinta and the others watched the man ride off to tell the others. Just then, Alinta noticed a second dust cloud, this one coming from the other track that led off towards their folds and Twin Station. She went up to Mel and asked, "Visitors?" She liked it when Mel put her arm around her, giving her a sideways hug. She liked the closeness and longed for more but didn't know how to ask.

"Yes. Dan said he saw them when he was hauling trees," she answered, mentioning the stockman who had run to gather others to help.

Alinta smiled. The name Dan meant something entirely different in her language, and she still found that amusing. These white names were sometimes hard to say, but this one was easy.

"Do you see dust over that way?" Mel's pointed with her chin towards the other track.

"Yes. More visitors?"

"I'm hoping it's Shamus O'Grady come to build our house and barns."

"What if he don't come?"

"What if he *doesn't* come?" Mel corrected automatically, shrugging philosophically. "Then, I guess we can make do with building on our own, but I'd rather have someone who knows what they are doing build things using our manpower." She wondered if Alinta understood all that.

"You build bunk," she stated, pointing with her own chin at the barracks the men had built, a trail of smoking rising from the chimney that went up the center of the building.

"The bunkhouse...er barracks," she corrected, "isn't a difficult building to put up, but the house, the barns, and the sheds are important for the future of the station."

They watched as the dust clouds came closer. The one directly to the south was becoming more visible, and the one to the southeast was much, much larger. Mel surmised that one contained the animals she had sent for. The sheep folds here at the home station were ready and could hold thousands of animals. The corrals for horses and cows and the pens for pigs hadn't been hard to build, and the men had been able to put those together for Mel. They'd run out of nails in their building efforts. There had been so many of those valuable pieces of metal that Alinta couldn't imagine they would ever run out. Mel had been about to send someone from the station with mail and have them also buy a keg or two of nails from Wilcannia. She wanted to go herself but didn't want to leave Alinta right before the rainy season, which was almost upon them. She looked out at the countryside, amazed that no one lived in this vast interior. It was a dry area, but where she had decided to build her home next to the hidden valley, she was sure it was going to be a paradise.

The beauty of the place and its splendor intrigued her daily. Alinta really enjoyed her almost nightly walks with her husband and daughter. Occasionally, they took horses, exploring north of the chosen homesite. Mel had plans for paddocks and folds up there as well when her flocks grew. Alinta didn't understand all her husband's plans, but she liked her enthusiasm and loved listening to her explanations as she made them. She just loved spending this quiet time together.

The larger cloud got closer, and Mel and Alinta could see the distant figures coming over the hills. It was then they saw the reason for the enormous cloud of dust coming up over the trees and hills. It was created by the row of carts they saw up front. Many, many carts were coming and behind them thousands of hoofs were churning the grasses to dust. The track had been well worn from dragging trees and was now flattened and compacted beyond anything Mel could have hoped to do herself. In many places the track had begun to grow back. Nature was taking it back with plants that had sporadically sprung up down the center between the paths of the wheels. Now, they were

trampled into nothingness as the animals continued to come and come. No wonder it had taken so long for them to arrive; it had been many, many months. It must have taken an extensive amount of time for her solicitor to find someone he could trust with the large order Mel had sent him, much less to find and purchase the animals and have them driven into the far Outback.

Mel let go of Alinta, kissing her before mounting her horse. She didn't rush as she headed down the hill, skirting the playful puppies on her way. She had been relieved when all the puppies birthed by the two bitches had shown an interest in sheep. She had personally pulled half a dozen sheep from one of the nearest folds just to test the pups. She kept the few wethers at the home paddocks for their family's consumption, and now, she used them to train the pups as they grew. One of the pups had been borderline interested in the sheep at first, and Mel had worried she would have to destroy him, but it had just taken him a little longer to realize what his siblings instinctively knew…sheep were to be herded. Alinta and a few of the stockmen had watched, fascinated, as the pups tried to herd the small flock of sheep. She could sense Mel's relief that they had all shown an interest in herding, and Mel explained she would have had to destroy the pups if they had not. Alinta thought it a waste that white people destroyed animals that weren't of immediate use to them.

Several men mounted their own horses and followed Mel as she rode out to meet the drovers. Alinta and the others left behind were excited. Some went to open the gates to the pens in anticipation of receiving the animals they could see coming down the track. The women, Alinta included, went back to working in the garden and were joined by a couple of the men as they expanded the garden by digging up more of the dirt. A long while later, Mel returned, and Alinta waved as she headed past the garden and up the second track towards the second dust cloud. Alinta was pleased to see Carmen, Fabiola, some of the men from their station, and the vaqueros. She was also surprised to see some aboriginal people in carts, who stared at her shamelessly. She followed them up to the corrals where people got out and stood looking around, and she was pleased when Carmen greeted her. Mel tied off her horse as she got down.

"Oh, let me see that baby," the Hispanic American said and held out her arms for the darling girl.

Alinta happily handed the baby to their friend, removing her from the sling she had fashioned to hold the sturdy baby, who now studied the dark-haired woman with her baby blue eyes. The baby's eyes hadn't turned dark like Alinta's, but their brightness fascinated the Aborigine. She likened them to the sky.

"It's good to see you," Fabiola told her, smiling, and a pleasantly surprised Alinta returned the smile. Fabiola walked over to where Mel watched the flocks of sheep and herds of animals as they were turning into the paddocks. Harold nodded to Alinta before walking off towards where the men were congregating. Already, boisterous laughter was coming from the barracks. "Whatever you do, don't let Shamus find your rum," Fabiola warned Mel quietly.

Mel turned to her, alarmed. "I was going to send some rum down for Braun and his men to celebrate the end of their long drive. They brought all these animals," her hands gestured, taking in the folds and paddocks they were filling. The many animals were already getting used to their new accommodations and settling down, many of them

eating the overgrown grasses that had continued to grow, disregarding the fences Mel and her men had erected.

Carmen came up, cuddling the baby and bouncing her a little. "That's why we came with him. Not only to see you both," her smile encompassed both Mel and Alinta, "but to make sure he got here in one piece. It took him much longer to build what we wanted because he and his men found our rum supply, and they were drunk half the time. For God's sake, keep your rum under lock and key."

Mel nodded, wanting to laugh but at the same time, knowing it really wasn't funny. There was a lot of work that had to be done, and the man had delayed it by months due to his drinking. She'd expected him to finish on Twin Station a long time ago. "I'll bet there's rum in those supplies," she said, nodding to the many carts that had come in from the southeast and were now being parked against the many corrals and sheep folds in a long, neat row.

"Lock it up," Fabiola warned her, repeating Carmen's warning. She was not amused. The man had nearly caused a fire with his carelessness, but she grudgingly acknowledged that when he was sober, he was one of the hardest working men she had ever known. The hacienda he had built for Carmen was beautiful. The barns were also first class, but they had taken much too long to build.

"Why they here?" Alinta pointed at the Aborigines standing about and looking lost. No one had said anything to them.

"I told them they could come here and there would be jobs if they wanted to live here. Is that okay?" Mel asked, suddenly concerned that her wife wouldn't want them here. They weren't her people, and she hadn't been able to communicate with the others when they were on Twin Station.

"Oh, most of them aren't from our station," Fabiola told Mel, much to her surprise. "Word spread, and they came with us when we decided to escort Shamus here."

"How did they know when you were leaving?" Mel asked, confused about how word had gotten about.

Fabiola shrugged and answered, "If you can tell me how they know things half the time, we will both have learned something. They are mysterious and at one with this land."

Mel nodded, curious about how they had heard, but Alinta had told her that an Aborigine could send messages over long distances and word would spread if they wanted something known. They also had ways of knowing that the elders passed on in secret. Mel didn't quite understand it, but she was certain her wife didn't understand a lot of what she tried to explain about white people either. Mel was still looking at Alinta, concerned that maybe she didn't want these people to live here on the station and waiting on her answer.

"Yes, okay," she said, her voice sounding odd as she looked at the dozen or so people standing there watching the white people interact. She glanced at the white women, who looked a little uncomfortable as they surveyed the unfinished place. They looked as though they were clustered together for protection.

"Why don't we go and introduce ourselves?" Mel jovially asked Carmen, Fabiola, and Alinta. "You can put your things down by our fire," she pointed to where Alinta had obviously started their dinner. She noted there was more food than usual by the fire, and she realized her wife must have known they would have guests.

"This is Mister Lawrence," Fabiola said to the new aboriginal people, slowly enunciating the name. "And this is her wife, Missus Lawrence."

Their eyes, especially the adults' eyes, went wide when they saw that Alinta was a full-blooded Aborigine but not of their tribe.

"Welcome. Thank you for coming. We can build you some houses along the creek–" Mel began, but her thought was interrupted when one of the elders made a sideways motion with his hand that she caught. Being around Alinta for so long, she was much more aware of these things than she had been.

"We build huts," he said in pidgin English.

"No, I would like you to have houses," Mel contradicted.

"Mel, they are fine in–" Fabiola began.

"I've seen their huts. Their huts are fine, if they are living in the bush. I would like them to have nice homes built of wood here," she insisted, having given this a lot of thought. She had asked Alinta if people like her own tribe or other tribes would like nice homes, and she hadn't been sure.

"Our huts fine," the man insisted.

"Yes, they are. Why don't we build both huts and houses for your people and let them choose?" Mel offered, and he smiled as he nodded agreeably. "Would you like to build them there?" she pointed along the creek, well away from where she would be building the stockmen's houses, so the Aborigines' village would have privacy. She knew some people would be prejudiced against these natives regardless of how hard they worked. "Do you need anything now?"

"Some tucker would probably go down good," Fabiola murmured helpfully.

"I'll send my men down with some food for you and your people," Mel offered, and the elder smiled appreciatively. "We can talk more after you get settled."

They watched as the group walked off in the direction Mel had indicated, carrying their meager possessions.

"You are going to have to be firm with them," Fabiola told her, mindful that Alinta was standing there and not wishing to insult their friend's wife. "A lot of Aborigines don't understand the concept of ownership. Have the men hunt dingoes and build things, but I've never seen a stockman who wasn't mixed. They just don't understand that the sheep aren't theirs to give away. Have the women work in the garden or train their girls to watch Ainia," she advised, smiling at Carmen who was still holding the little bundle.

Remembering that Fabiola and Harold's mother had been an Aborigine, Mel was surprised. "I'm sure they can learn if they want–" Mel began and was amazed when Alinta disagreed with her.

"Some won't learn. Won't give up the old ways. They want to keep *their* ways. They take your tucker. Hunt dingoes. Won't live in house."

Mel smiled at her wife and shrugged. "Well, all we can do is try," she promised as she left to welcome the stockmen's wives, who were looking about and appeared quite lost. "Hello. I'm Mel Lawrence, and this is my wife, Alinta...Missus Lawrence," she said by way of introduction as she put her arm around the shorter woman. Alinta could see the change in the women's eyes when they saw her. "We'll have houses up for the married stockmen in a few days. Meanwhile, you will have to make do as you did on the trek out here." Several

agreed gracefully, but Alinta could see a couple were annoyed and wondered at that.

They enjoyed their evening around the fire, talking about the stock Mel had brought in with their friends. Braun joined them for a time, talking knowledgeably about the stock and supplies he had brought but obviously anxious to head back to civilization as soon as possible. A few of his drovers would leave with him but most had come to hire on, and Mel welcomed their presence. Already, her men were planning on dividing up the new sheep and making new folds out in the bush, several along the track she had made towards the southeast. She knew several places where she wanted to place them but only after the enormous work force she had at the home station helped put up the barns, the stables, the sheds, and especially, the house. She only hoped the rains would hold off long enough that they could accomplish some of what she was planning. Alinta listened, taking in what she could and making notes in her head to ask Mel about the words she didn't understand. She enjoyed visiting with their friends and loved that she was included, even if she didn't understand all their words.

CHAPTER FOUR

Alinta watched in awe as the barns went up. So many men made short work of the enormous stacks of wood that Mel and the other men had put by for the various projects. She didn't understand what block and tackle was, but she gleaned that it helped the men to lift very heavy pieces of wood into place. She looked at the cavernous buildings that were going up, trying to understand the need for so much enclosed space. Mel explained that the style of one barn was called Monitor and the other barn was Gambrel, showing her the dormers and gables. While they were pretty, they meant nothing to the aboriginal woman, but Alinta realized Mel needed to talk and explain, so she listened patiently as her wife spoke. She liked that some of the floors in the barns were made of wood and some were made of stone that felt good

on her bare feet. The dirt on some of the floors especially felt real to her as she examined these immense buildings.

The thing that impressed Alinta the most were the sheets of metal that they put on the roofs of the buildings. Her father would not have believed that so much of the coveted white man's stone existed, and they were using it on the roofs of various barns and sheds. The metal had been flattened into sheets with grooves that would help shed the rain, and it was being affixed to the wooden frames of the roof. Mel had arranged for lots of metal to be shipped in for her buildings, and it was carried in the many carts that had arrived. She explained that metal roofs would help the buildings to last a very long time.

There were windows at the top of the shearing shed, enabling plenty of light to streak into the large building. After having witnessed a season of shearing already, Alinta understood how important it was for the men to see the sheep as they removed the wool. They would be able to shear so long as there was daylight.

Next, some of the men put up the many stockmen's houses that Mel wanted. Anyone with a wife and children could use them. They were erected on wood that Mel called stilts. They were like the houses Alinta had seen on Twin Station, able to keep bugs out and high enough that the waters of the creek wouldn't creep into the structures. She liked that it was shady and cool down here near the creek, and Mel explained that she was having bathtubs installed in each house. Alinta understood the words bath and tub individually but not when used together. She now took regular baths because Mel wanted it, and she washed Ainia at the same time, but a tub was something she used to gather things. It was all very confusing to the woman, who had no

point of reference. Then, Mel showed her that you could also wash clothes in a bathtub, and she thought she understood now.

A well was dug nearby their house. This reminded Alinta of the holes that she and her mother had dug so long ago, reaching the strata where her mother knew water was hidden in the desert. The difference was, they wouldn't be filling this hole back in with the dirt and stones they dug out. They dug down what Mel told her was over forty feet. Alinta loved the cool, fresh water. It was delicious. Mel promised they would have running water in their house, and Alinta smiled. She had no idea what that meant, but Mel was excited by the idea, and O'Grady, the builder, said he knew how to hook it up.

O'Grady made great fires and plastered the mud they called clay around thin trees, which he burned in the fires. When the wood burned to ash, it left behind long tubes that Mel said were called pipes, and these pipes would be used to draw water in or out of the house as they needed.

The main house would have *two* bathrooms, one for the master bedroom and one for the rest of the house, and again, Alinta smiled and nodded, wondering about this. She would have to wait and see what her husband meant, and she looked forward to it since it excited the large woman so.

The stockmen's houses were only halfway built when their friends, Carmen and Fabiola insisted it was time for them to return to their own station. Mel and Alinta would miss them, having enjoyed their visit immensely. Their friends had pitched in with everyone else, and they too were amazed at the beautiful buildings O'Grady had designed based on Mel's ideas and how quickly they had gone up.

Mel thanked Carmen and Fabiola for their help and for the men who had come with them. Both she and Alinta waved them on their way. Alinta would miss Carmen's help in caring for her small baby. Carmen had doted on the little girl that was growing like a weed. Their friends had given them well over a week of help, and Mel appreciated it, but she knew they had just as much work as she had waiting for them on their own station with the oncoming rainy season. She was puzzled by the fact that Howard had come with them, but she hadn't seen him do anything other than socialize with the men. She wondered what he really did and was glad he was leaving.

Alinta could smell the rain on the breeze as the dark clouds massed above them and on the horizon. The squalls they had gotten helped the grasses and the garden, but it was nothing like what would come during the rainy season that was nearly upon them. She knew Mel was worried about all the building that remained to be done.

Mel had asked O'Grady to put pipes in each of the stockmen's houses too, utilizing his technique to make the clay pipes and give the stockmen fresh water from the tanks they put up under the shady trees. She wanted to do the same for the small aboriginal village that had gone up downstream, but Alinta vetoed that idea. She explained that too many of the white man's conveniences might scare the natives off. Mel acquiesced but still planned to put in small houses that she hoped they would eventually use, and she planned that these would have fresh water.

Alinta watched, amazed as Mel not only worked on the various buildings but also helped to sort their animals. She sent one stockman down the track with a flock, heading back towards the southeast and the one unoccupied fold they had built there. Mel sent him off with only one thousand sheep, his dogs, and a pack animal carrying a measured amount of supplies. Mel had explained that the home station wouldn't support this many animals with all the grazing they were already doing and how they were mowing the grasses about the place. She sent many of them down into the hidden valley to graze on the luxuriant grasses that grew there and left only a limited number of domesticated animals on the fields.

As the clouds massed, the men hurried to finish the shell of the main house, giving Mel a structure to live in since everyone else already had either the barracks or a house. Mel had considered moving into one of the well-built sheds or barns but hadn't liked that idea and hoped they still had time to get more work done on their house. They moved into one corner of the large, unfinished building—where the kitchen was located—just as the first real storm of the season hit. The winds were terrible, and they battered the house, but the three of them were snug and cozy next to the small fire Mel had taught Alinta to build in the stove. There were other fixtures in the kitchen that amazed the aboriginal woman as Mel made them meals and taught Alinta how to use things.

The white man's stone was utilized in many ways, and Alinta rubbed it admiringly while thinking of how envious her people would be of the riches available to her now. Sometimes, she wondered where her family was, although she knew that Omeo, her father, wasn't wondering about her. She thought her mother, Inala, would have loved to hold and spoil Ainia, and she pondered what kind of woman her brother, Miro, would find someday. She often watched the Aborigines who lived along the creek and were making a village for themselves. The conical huts called wurlies went up quickly and were well built

despite Mel's concerns. Alinta knew her husband intended to build houses for the Aborigines. They would not be as luxurious as the stockmen's houses; they would be simpler and just as nice. She was astonished at this house they now lived in. It was huge and still unfinished. She didn't understand everything yet, but Mel promised to explain anything she wanted to know. There was the wonder of the glass windows and being able to look beyond the walls of their house without bugs coming in. And Alinta was amazed at the pump that provided fresh water in their kitchen sink. She was used to fetching water from a creek or a billabong when she needed it, and she knew the urn she had made so long ago would have been useless in this white man's world. Alinta knew she wanted to live in Mel's world, and her *husband,* as Mel had requested she refer to her, seemed to need these things about her/him. Alinta was learning so much, and there was still so much she didn't comprehend, so she stayed quiet and observed. She saw some of the married stockmen and their wives embracing each other, even doing that mouth on mouth thing she had so enjoyed with Mel. She wanted more of that for herself and Mel, but she wasn't sure how to broach the subject. Alinta wasn't one to initiate conversation or contact with Mel. She would wait and see what more might develop between them when Mel decided it was time. She trusted the big woman with the manliness inside her. Something about that manliness excited her although she couldn't quite put her finger on it.

There was always so much work to do, and Mel was always tired. She had known the work would be never-ending, but she was young, and her body was able to adjust to it. She spent her evenings quietly with Alinta and their daughter, enjoying the peacefulness. There was so much more Mel wanted once Ainia was fed and asleep, but she had hesitated for so long and didn't know how to change their routine. At first, she had waited for Alinta to heal, and later, she had waited for them to find time to be alone together. Now, they were finally alone in their own house, and she impulsively kissed Alinta one night before sleep. This evening kiss was a practice she had used to help Alinta become familiar with her touch, but that night everything changed. Alinta never discouraged her husband, and Mel wondered what Alinta might do if she took things further. Mel deepened the kiss, exploring the woman's mouth with her lips and tongue and scenting her wife's fresh, natural odors with her senses.

Alinta had always enjoyed the mouth on mouth kiss that Mel gave her once she understood that it was a sign of affection. As Mel used her tongue and encouraged Alinta to use hers, she began to explore Mel's mouth, tasting the flavor of her. She didn't understand when both their breathing increased, but the petting that Mel bestowed on her body felt good, and she copied it, exploring the big woman's body.

Mel loved the feel of Alinta's strong and supple fingers on her body. Her wife's touch was at first, hesitant, then became bolder. Slowly, they began to remove each other's clothing. Alinta copied whatever Mel did.

Mel's wraps got in the way after a while, so they quickly removed them, and Alinta rubbed around her husband's sides where the wraps seemed to have caused redness on her body. Mel seemed to enjoy the rubbing too, and Alinta wanted to please her.

Naked bodies were something Alinta had seen her entire life but seeing the muscular Mel naked was overwhelming to her senses. Of course, she'd glimpsed things during the time they had been together, but she had learned at an early age to avert her eyes and not to stare at

others. Now, in the flickering firelight of the stove, she was enjoying the play of light on the white woman's large body. She wanted that body against her. She wanted to feel that body holding her down and making her feel as though she were helpless. Her breathing continued to increase as they kissed and touched, and that puzzled her. Remembering her parents' couplings, she wondered if this feeling of breathlessness was why they did it. She also wondered if she would end up with that same vacant look in her eyes as her mother had or if she would feel the intense emotion that seemed to come over her father. She quashed all thoughts of her parents and concentrated on Mel.

Alinta loved the contrast of her fingers against Mel's body. Alinta looked so dark against the white skin under Mel's clothes that had never seen a day of sunlight. The contrast of their bodies fascinated her, and she loved the effect it was having on the American woman. Alinta touched everywhere she could reach, copying what Mel was doing to her body and enjoying giving the sensations as well as receiving them. She had never thought that a caress could make her feel so good, but it wasn't just any caress or touch, it was Mel's caress and touch.

Slowly, the two women explored, going much further than they had in the past months as they got to know each other's bodies. As Mel gently played around the breasts that fed their daughter, she saw milk forming. She avoided the tips she so badly wanted to lick and suckle, not wanting to deny their daughter the nourishment. She hoped that someday, when Alinta stopped feeding, the breasts would dry up and she could teach her wife the enjoyment that could be attained by her lover licking and sucking on them. Instead, she continued nuzzling across the taut belly, noting the few stretch marks from her pregnancy

and then moving lower to the small bush of hair, tickling and watching her wife's reaction to her touch. Mel encouraged Alinta to spread her legs, inserting her own leg between them to rub gently at the Y.

Alinta had rarely touched herself there and had never imagined she'd enjoy being touched there by another human being. Mel seemed to find pleasure in the moisture that came from her body. Much to her surprise, the feel of the bigger woman's thigh between her legs made her grind against it slightly, and she felt the primitive need of it as they continued.

Mel smiled against the belly she was kissing, her fingers entwining in the hairs and the folds that had become so odorous and wet beneath her. As she explored, she heard the intake of Alinta's breath when her fingers touched the nerve endings and rubbed. Slowly and firmly, she brushed up and down the slit, noting the moisture increased and was almost sousing the palm of her hand. Mel knew Alinta wasn't yet ready for too many intimacies even though her own mouth was watering in anticipation of the taste. The odors she sensed were telling her how good it would be. Mel desperately wanted to taste there but would save that for another time. Instead, her fingers continued to explore and give her wife pleasure, one creeping inside to see how the wild woman reacted.

This wasn't at all like that man's invasion of her body, and Alinta enjoyed the feel of Mel inside her. She welcomed it. When Mel's one finger became two and they curled slightly, Alinta was in shock at the sensations that pulsed in her body, and she became limp when Mel hit her G spot. Alinta hadn't known she had these feelings inside her or that a simple touch could affect her so. Mel expertly played her body, and she couldn't have resisted if she wanted to…she certainly didn't

want the woman to stop. She wanted more, and her fingers pulled at Mel's shoulders, encouraging her as she ground down against her.

Mel began to pump, her thumb plying the nubbin of flesh that had risen on the outside, her fingers at first stiff and straight, then bending slightly to find the sentient flesh within. She could tell Alinta's passions were building by listening to the anguished breathing and feeling the claw-like fingers on her shoulders and the grinding against her hand and leg. Mel was becoming more and more excited as she realized the passions that had previously laid dormant in her wild wife. She pumped harder, making sure to hit her wife's G spot and rub the clit that was standing up more prominently than before.

At the time of crisis, the first time she had ever experienced this in her life, Alinta's primitive instincts came to the forefront, and she ended up biting Mel's shoulder, totally unaware that she had done so.

Mel couldn't believe the passions she saw displayed before her. She felt the pain of Alinta's teeth as they bruised and broke the skin on her shoulder, but she didn't stop as she drove her wife higher and higher, her lips sucking on skin and making hickies as she continued to pump her wife and listen to her cries, exciting herself as she made her wife come. Mel moved up, brushing the teeth from her shoulder as she covered Alinta's body with her own. She watched her wife come undone with what she suspected was her first ever orgasm. Little cries escaped from the smaller woman's mouth, building as she reached her crises, and Mel quickly kissed her to capture the roar of completion that unknowingly escaped from the woman. She arched her body, her legs clasping Mel's hand between them almost painfully. In the aftermath, as the woman writhed beneath her, Mel kept her warm with her heated and sweaty body, enjoying the little spasms that squeezed her fingers.

"Are you okay?" Mel asked a while later as she pulled a blanket over their naked bodies. She glanced at Ainia to make sure they hadn't woken the baby, but she was still sleeping, her lips moving as though she were suckling as she dreamed.

"Ya, okay," Alinta whispered back, touching her fingers wonderingly as they tingled, and the blood returned. She had never known such a feeling, and it unnerved her. She opened her eyes and looked up at Mel, who was looking down at her with love and tenderness as she held her in the light projected by the fire in the stove. Alinta looked away bashfully, and Mel held her closer, understanding what she was too shy to say.

CHAPTER FIVE

Mel returned to building folds for the many sheep they now possessed, and Alinta watched as she rode away with the crews that would be helping her. Mel had explained that she would use the excess men they had before many returned to civilization. Some of the men continued working at the home paddock, on the houses, or on the barns.

Daily, Alinta watched in puzzlement as they continued putting up walls in the big house that Mel had them building. Living in the kitchen, she didn't understand the different things they were doing, but found it fascinating, and she continued watching while trying not to make it obvious. A couple of the workers had complained to Mel that Alinta was always about and watching. Mel discussed it with them and determined that it wasn't about her wife's skin color or their racism, so she explained to them that the aboriginal woman had a childlike interest

in what they were doing because she had never seen a house built before. She mentioned it to Alinta, so she wouldn't be as obvious when watching them.

Alinta had chores to do, which took her and the baby out to the barn. The chickens were laying eggs, which she had to gather, and she was sharing them with the other women at the home paddock. There were a lot of times when she didn't know what to do with herself now that she couldn't work in the garden with the pouring rain, but the rain didn't seem to stop Mel and her crews from building inside or out. Alinta would have gone with them, but Mel asked her to keep Ainia warm, dry, and safe at the home paddock. She wanted to be with Mel, but her maternal instincts were at war with her wants.

Mel returned from the paddocks where she was trying to save the sheep and get them to high ground. As she dismounted her horse, a snake struck at her. Only the fact that she was wearing knee-high boots prevented the snake from striking her leg. Mel calmly shot the snake, and several people came running, including Alinta, who had been watching for her wife.

"You okay?" Alinta walked up, holding the baby and looking concerned.

"Have I ever mentioned I *hate* snakes?" Mel grinned wryly, looking down at her pant leg where the snake had struck and seeing a hole in her trousers.

Alinta was smiling in response to the joking note in Mel's voice, but she lost her smile when she saw the tear in the pants' leg. "He bite you?" she asked, suddenly worried and feeling vulnerable as she looked around for more snakes.

"No, he got the leather of my boots, that is all," Mel reassured her, taking her and the baby in her arms in a hug.

"What would we do without you?" Alinta murmured against her shirt. Since they had made love several times now, Alinta had learned to love on a level she hadn't known existed. The physical pleasure this woman gave her was like nothing she had come to expect. She hadn't been sure when Mel indicated she wanted more from her physically, but all her fears had been put to rest. She looked forward to what more she would learn from this woman.

Mel pulled back to look down on the smaller woman. "I've made arrangements if anything were to happen to me. You and Ainia would be taken care of as my heirs," Mel informed her. "But I hope that won't happen for a long time in the future. We have a lot to build here," her hand gestured at the home paddock and out to the land beyond, "and I'm looking forward to a long life with you."

Alinta smiled. She didn't understand what Mel meant by taking care of them, and she didn't know what an heir was, but she pleased to hear that Mel wanted a long life with her. She'd never had a friend, and Mel assured her she thought of her as her best friend, her mate, and her love. She liked the love part now that she understood it better.

Mel had to let some of the men return to Sydney now that much of the work they had been hired for was done. She explained to Alinta that they had an excess of carts, and she allowed the men to take several to use as they headed back from the Outback. Some of the men were on horses, but they would travel slowly as the bullocks pulling the

carts could only plod along. With the rain, it would be a miserable trip, but at least they were heading back to civilization. Some of them were relieved they were done. Braun, the man Mel had paid off for the long trip, received a packet of letters enclosed in a waterproof wrap that Mel wanted mailed for her. A couple letters would be hand-delivered to Saunders, her solicitor, and while Alinta didn't know what a solicitor or a lawyer was, she knew the man must be important to Mel.

Alinta was fascinated by the letter writing. One of the men had made them a kitchen table and chairs, and Mel taught her to read and write sitting at this table. Alinta tried to memorize everything as quickly as Mel showed it her, earning smiles from her husband as she patiently showed her how to copy what she was doing. She watched in envy as Mel wrote rapidly and compiled her letters. Alinta wondered what she would communicate across the vast distances in such a clever way.

Mel had other duties that kept her going out to the paddocks as the men worked in them, and Alinta always welcomed her home each time she rode back in.

"I would like to ride with you sometime," Alinta mentioned She was finding caring for the chickens, the ducks, and the garden between rain squalls to be boring. She was a familiar figure with her gathering stick, which she used to kill snakes, scorpions, and anything else that threatened them or their livestock. She feared little. Ainia was a handful but calmed when she rode on a horse in front of her mother. She was thrilled to see Mel and wanted to ride with her too. It was becoming harder as Mel was going farther afield to get the folds done and was gone a lot, despite the rain. She wanted to get the men onto the other folds north of their location and get them ready with the natural increases of their flocks but knew that would have to wait. One of the letters she had sent out was a request for someone to start fencing for her. She simply didn't have enough men to do all that work. She wanted Outback men that weren't afraid of the vastness, and she also wanted to start enclosing her paddocks, so they didn't lose sheep. She'd explained all this to Alinta, stopping to elaborate further when she used words the woman didn't understand. Some of it she would simply have to show her since she didn't have words or explanations for some of her ideas, and Alinta had no comprehension since they didn't do things like that in her world.

"You want to go out to the folds with me?"

Alinta nodded, watching her husband carefully. She didn't want to sit in the big empty house that was now essentially completed except for the furniture that would have to wait until more carts came all the way from Sydney. They were living in the kitchen, which was nice and warm, but Alinta preferred to be outdoors, and only a few of the stockmen's wives associated with her since she was the owner's wife. She knew others didn't like her because she was an Aborigine. They hid their prejudices well, pleased that their husbands had work and not willing to jeopardize their positions, but Alinta knew. She could sense it in the way they behaved or spoke to her. She didn't care, not really understanding prejudice. What she didn't know was, her husband was aware of their disdain, and if anything came of it, Mel was ready to deal with it. So far, their husbands had proven to be good workers, or she would have sent them on their way back to Sydney with Braun and his other men.

Mel was trying to be fair to her wife as she knew she couldn't have sat at the house either. She had traditional ideas of the role of a wife, and her wife seemed to fit none of them. Alinta was a wild thing, used to being outdoors and very independent. She couldn't put her in a mold. Mel smiled, indicating that she was going to give her wife favorable news. "Sure, anytime you want to go, you can just saddle up and get Ainia ready," she promised. One of the letters she had sent was an ad for people who could work in the Outback. She was not only looking for stockmen but also help in the house. Alinta was a lot cleaner than she had been. She didn't allow the dirt to build up on her person anymore, bathing regularly since Mel had shown her how much she liked it, but she still wouldn't be able to keep the house in the way Mel wanted. Mel had lived in the dirt long enough, and while she hadn't minded it as they traveled the vast Outback, now she wanted her home to be a sanctuary, and there was no way a primitive woman growing up in the Outback of Australia could understand the white man's ways or standards of upkeep that Mel expected. The furniture and other items Mel had ordered would need to be maintained, cleaned, and kept nice. The only way Alinta could learn these standards was if she were shown, and barring a trip to Sydney, which Mel knew would cause her wife endless anxiety over the amount of time she would be gone, there was only one way to show her. Mel would have to find people to create the house she wanted and maintain it.

Some of the men were still building stalls, furniture, and other things in the barn that they would need when the sheep were sheared in the spring. Alinta watched, fascinated, as they created things that filled her with wonder. Some of the things she remembered from being on Twin Station, and she nodded as she helped place them in the barns and sheds. She kept Ainia wrapped in her sling and safely tucked against her to free both her hands.

"That rain is something else," Mel marveled, watching the flooding that was inundating the creeks. The dams they had erected were far under water, and she was worrying that they had been washed away.

"Have to make up when it's dry all summer," Alinta philosophized and Mel grinned. Her wife was a very wise woman.

"I have to remember that as we make folds farther north where it's drier," Mel murmured as she thought about the next project she wanted the men to tackle.

Soon enough, their winter was over, and they looked forward to the lambing. They hoped it wouldn't be as intense as the last year when they were alone with all those birthing sheep. Fortunately, the flocks were much smaller and spread out in the various paddocks and folds.

"I wish I knew when those flocks from Sydney were due to give birth," Mel griped, annoyed that the men bringing them out had allowed the rams in among the unprotected sheep. They could give birth anytime. She'd explained her worries to Alinta, not wishing to share them with her men, who were probably already worried about all that extra work. Alinta was the only one that Mel could confide in, and since she often didn't understand the worry or why it was a problem, Mel didn't worry too much about burdening her.

As the sheep began to give birth, Mel had one flock brought into the home paddock, and she sent men out to help in the various folds. Dingoes were a problem in each of the paddocks, and extra men could help keep the sheep and their offspring safe. Alinta still hated the sound of the guns as it always startled her, but Mel was absolutely

thrilled when one of the stockmen got a dozen dingoes strung up by their tails and hanging from the trees. She gave the man a bonus, explaining to Alinta that this was extra money. She said word of this would spread to the other men in the other paddocks and give them an incentive to kill even more of the predators.

Mulesing and docking the sheep was more difficult in some cases due to the different breeds. The job was up to the individual stockmen, but Mel and the others she sent out to help pitched in as well. Even Alinta helped this year with Ainia strapped to her back when she could or toddling about at other times. They kept an eye on the little girl, so a dingo wouldn't get her. They knew the dingo wouldn't discriminate between the young of a sheep or the young of a human. Mel made sure she was always nearby to protect their daughter when Ainia was on the ground.

CHAPTER SIX

Alinta watched as the shearers arrived from Twin Station with letters from Carmen and Fabiola. She remembered some of the men from the previous year and saw them looking with awe at the new, clean buildings. She understood that feeling herself. The buildings didn't remain clean for long once all the sheep were brought in to be sheared.

Alinta followed Mel and listened to the talk about sheep, not completely understanding it but learning as the men joked and talked.

"Some station near Cobar is trying to raise them sheep that have hair instead of wool," one of the shearers mentioned, never stopping his chatter as he worked the shears effortlessly.

"Hair? Not wool? How do you shear them?" another asked, his unlit pipe in the corner of his mouth. Mel wouldn't allow smoking

anywhere near the barns or sheds, insisting it be confined to the barracks and the hall.

"You don't," said the first shearer. "They shed like dogs or cats."

The others guffawed, sure he was funning them, but Mel had heard of sheep like this and wondered about them. "What happens if you breed 'em to wool-bearing sheep?"

The man eyed the Yank station owner for a second. "I bet you'd have to shear them," he answered. "I hain't seen 'em though, only heard about 'em."

That kind of talk was how rumors were spread, and the men took it with a grain of salt, thinking it was a tall tale like the stories of bunyips and other bush stories.

"I bet them hair sheep ain't any good for spinnin'," another shearer put in.

"Bet I can shear the most sheep today," another challenged in order to get more work out of his men. All of them took on the challenge.

Mel smiled, a good sheep shearer could shear a sheep in less than two minutes and remove the entire fleece in one piece. Stompers were the men who collected the fleeces, put them in the large bags, and stomped on the bags to pack them full of the various fleeces. The stompers were kept busy!

"I heard one man sheared eight hundred sheep in just nine hours," one man commented.

"Bullshit!" several voices rang out in protest. They knew the most they could hope for was fifty sheep a day by a shearer using hand blades.

Mel grinned at their good-natured ribbing and slightly competitive natures. She'd shorn a few sheep herself, realizing she was outclassed by these quickly efficient men. She wouldn't compete with them; there was no reason to. They did a good job, although occasionally, a newer man would nick one of her sheep and get a ration of shit from his buddies over it. She liked that they seemed determined not to nick her sheep, who looked so helpless as they were stripped of their winter jackets.

"What is hair on sheep instead of wool?" Alinta asked her husband later, proving she had been listening. Mel delighted in explaining it to her wife, using her fingers to show her as she finger-combed Alinta's tresses, creating a sensual and erotic feel between them as she explained. This led to more pleasant things, and they delighted in each other.

Alinta collected plants and made up a mixture that would help treat the sunburn on some sheep's newly exposed skin. Mel asked her wife to make it in large quantities as the scabs that formed on the poor sheep's skin disgusted her. "Get some of that mixture my wife made up on that lot there," she ordered the stockmen. Some of the men objected, but because Mel was the boss, they grudgingly did the extra work. Mel later explained to Alinta that some men just wanted to reap the profit from the sheep and didn't care about the sheep's well-being. Mel couldn't stand to see the sheep suffer for no good reason.

Mel had appointed a stockman named Peter as head stockman. She had him separating some of the sheep as she now regretted mixing the Merinos with the Leicester and other breeds of sheep. Most of the sheep looked the same to Alinta, but she could pick out the Leicester by their big ears. She watched as the sheep were released among the noisy lambs, who had been calling for their mothers as they were being

shorn. It was amazing how fast they found their lambs among all those babies.

The stacks of wool were building up. Full sacks now reached to the rafters as the sheep continued to be shorn. This no longer bothered Alinta, who remembered the men who had captured her. That was long ago, and she was glad to have Ainia as a result. Mel treated her so much better, and she loved her. She didn't think about Bradley or those other carters who had captured her. Mel was Ainia's father, and everyone else seemed to accept that as fact. Alinta wouldn't let the past enter their treasured relationship.

Mel paid off the shearers in cash money, not wool as so many other grazers or stations did. The men were thrilled with this arrangement and agreed to come to Lawrence Station first next year and go on to Twin Station afterward.

"I hope that doesn't create a problem with Carmen and Fabiola," Mel mentioned as she watched them heading off down the track and back to civilization, the money burning a hole in their pockets.

"Problem?" Alinta asked, leaning against her husband and watching the men leave.

"Hard feelings," Mel clarified, putting her arm around the much shorter woman.

It was a couple weeks later that the drays containing the much-needed supplies Mel was expecting finally made it to the station. She'd been expecting them right after the shearers left, but she supposed the distance they had to travel to get there was delaying them. Mel had also confided in Alinta about the vast sums of money she had been going through in her desire to build up the large station. While Alinta

had no concept of the money aspect, she knew it worried Mel, and she tried to be understanding.

"Men come?" Alinta asked as she pointed with her chin down the track while she played with Ainia on the lawn that Mel kept in front of the house. The rains had provided them with luxuriant growth, and Mel had been cutting the grass back with a scythe, finally assigning that task to one of the stockmen's sons. She also gave other children work to do around the home paddock. The children must learn to be useful, and she had talked to Peter Winston as well as Alinta about someday having a school at the station for both the white children and the Aborigines. Mel told Alinta that Ainia could have a tutor if she wanted, but the aboriginal woman wasn't quite sure what a tutor was. Mel tried to explain, but Alinta had never heard of such a thing, and she wasn't going to worry about it now since Ainia was still too young for that according to Mel.

"Yes, I think it's our supplies for the house," Mel said, squinting. She had also sent away for reading glasses, annoyed that her vision was worsening as she got older and was making it harder to read the letters and brochures she got in the mail.

The men began to unload the carts. Mel directed the furniture into the house, telling Alinta to show them where each item was to be placed in the house. Since Alinta didn't know what some of the furniture was, Mel told her where it went in a whisper, so she could direct the men and look like she knew what she was talking about. Charlie Oscar, the man in charge of the stockrooms, directed the supplies into the stockrooms, marking them against the manifest that had accompanied the drayage company.

"Sir, I believe this is yours," the head carter presented a box to Mel. "I was instructed to make sure I handed it directly to the station owner."

"Granger?" Mel exclaimed. "George Granger?" she asked, recognizing the man.

"Mel? Mel Lawrence!" he returned, smiling. "I thought the name was familiar, but I wasn't sure."

Mel shook the man's hand as he set the slatted box down. It smelled a little gamy, and a hissing noise could be heard coming from inside. "Is that my cat?" she asked, worried. "Where's the other one?"

"Yes, she's an ornery cuss and pregnant, as you requested, I understand," he said, sounding put out. "The male escaped, and I think something got him." He sounded sorry but had thought it odd to be transporting felines.

She nodded ruefully over the loss of the tomcat. "If the snakes don't get her and her kittens, we will have something else besides snakes to go after the mice and rats. I hate those things," she said, shuddering.

He laughed, understanding Mel's fear of snakes. A lot of the men hated snakes. "I thought it an odd request, but now, I understand," he said, indicating the cat.

"Let's put her in the shade on the porch, so she's out of the way and downwind," Mel said as she went to pick up the box. "Did you let her out on the trip?"

"Many times, but I almost lost her a couple times, and she kept shitting in there, so I couldn't keep up," he admitted. "She's been well fed, but she's a bitch, if you don't mind my sayin'."

Mel laughed, charmed by the idea that the cat was mean. "It's good to see you again, and I hope the trip wasn't too arduous. We have the wool all stacked and ready for your men once the carts are empty. If you need more carts, I have a few I can sell you too," Mel informed him as they put the cat on the porch and then headed down the steps, standing aside to allow room for some men that were bringing in a bedstead. Alinta was smiling happily. She had recognized what it was from Mel's descriptions. She knew where one of those went. After all, they had six bedrooms upstairs, and the key word in that descriptive was bed.

"Is that the girl you gambled with Bradley for?" George asked before he thought it through, surprised to see her looking so…good.

"Careful there, Granger. That's my wife, Alinta," Mel warned, feeling prickly at hearing the name Bradley, the man who had abused Alinta so. She supposed she owed him a debt for fathering Ainia, but she didn't want anyone to know that she wasn't the toddler's natural father. She didn't feel that anyone needed to know that. She saw the toddler standing there, staring at the commotion, a puppy that she had been playing with at her feet. She wondered how her daughter would react to kittens when they arrived.

"Oh, yes. Of course," he said, backing off immediately. What might be said about a slattern would certainly earn him a punch on the nose if it was said about a wife, and he wasn't even sure it was the same woman. This one looked him in the eye and appeared confident, and that other woman—he didn't remember if she even had a name— had looked downtrodden, dirty, and sickly to him. This woman wore proper clothes, her hair was combed, and she was very clean. Now that

he really thought about it, the other woman had been a mere girl, and this was a *real woman*.

"Let's get a move on with those supplies. I'm sure you are anxious to begin your return trip," she hinted broadly, distracting him.

George took the hint. He *was* anxious to get going. He hoped to hit another one or two stations on the long trip back to Sydney, depending on the amount of wool he collected and the number of carts he had left. He had liked hearing that Lawrence had some carts he was willing to part with. He might take him up on the offer since he had extra men with him who could drive the carts, and this would give him room to collect more wool. He glanced at the blonde-haired, blue-eyed, little girl with her finger in her mouth. She was watching the men move about and emptying the carts, and then, he saw Lawrence pick her up. She looked so much like the man that he immediately dismissed any thought that the child could belong to that slave girl from long ago. Besides, he didn't think an aboriginal woman could have birthed a child that looked so white.

"Mr. Lawrence?" Another man approached Mel as she spoke with her daughter and pointed out the animals to her.

Alinta came up and listened as Mel discussed with the man about building fences. She understood fences after all the folds they had built. She knew they were used to keep the sheep in an enclosed area. She continued to direct the men bringing in furniture as Mel talked to the other man, stopping only to whisper now and again to her husband about where a piece might go. Alinta avoided the man named Granger. She recognized who he was, and while she wasn't afraid of him, he brought back unpleasant memories.

Mel spotted the handsome, mahogany bedroom set she had ordered and smiled at the man carrying it. "That goes in the master bedroom," she told him as Alinta hurried to show him where that was. The last bed had gone in a spare bedroom; all Alinta knew was it went in a bedroom. She knew what master bedroom meant though, even if they had been living in the kitchen. She still didn't know what a kitchen was and had forgotten to ask Mel.

That night, the Aborigine village set up a corroboree, their digeridoos, drums, and dancing drawing others from the station as they all celebrated the arrival of the supplies. Mel allowed the men some rum, putting the rest of those supplies in the basement of the house to keep most of it under lock and key. There was a limited supply in the stockroom that Charley maintained for Mel. Each man got a share with his supplies when they were restocked.

Mel watched the men enjoying themselves as she and Alinta walked down. Ainia was on Alinta's hip, and Mel compared her to the pure aboriginal children, noting how much lighter her daughter was. Alinta also looked at the other children, noting that these people were much darker than her own tribe. She realized Ainia was lighter because of the man who had given her the child, her father's genes obviously being prevalent, but sometimes, in the right light, Alinta also looked white in profile. Even Alinta's hair wasn't as tight and springy as these aboriginal people. Ainia's hair was blonde, but aboriginal children were usually blonde until they got older and it changed. They had no idea if Ainia's hair would remain that light.

The headman, Djalu, approached Mel when he saw them watching the Aborigines' dancing and music playing.

"Good evening, Djalu," Mel said respectfully, knowing she had the name right as Alinta had helped her work on her pronunciation.

"Misster Lawwrrence," the man said deferentially, his pronunciation of the American name showing he had put in as much practice as she had to pronounce his correctly.

"Any of your men want some work? We are going out in two days to build fences," Mel told him. The men had helped around the home paddock, and a few of the boys were becoming jackaroos or apprentice stockmen, but both Peter Winston and Alinta had doubts about whether they could be taught. Mel was still hopeful that if they were taught young, they could grow up and learn to be good stockmen.

The man nodded to show he understood her question. Mel would pay them in supplies, and he had a fondness for the sweets they sometimes had in those supplies. The children almost had to fight the old man for their fair share when Mel doled out the sweets. He would tell the men about this work opportunity, and those that were interested could join them. He looked curiously at Ainia, wondering at the child of mixed races.

Mel and Alinta headed back to the main house as the mosquitos down by the creek were ferocious. "If we could only get rid of the flies and mosquitos," Mel complained as she increased her stride to get back up the hill and away from the water where they bred. Still, they followed her in the tall grasses, and the flies overwhelmed them during the day.

"I make mix," Alinta told her, referring to the plants she ground together that seemed to repel the bugs that the white men were so plagued with. The bugs didn't bother Alinta nearly as much except after she bathed.

"I'd appreciate it," Mel said, slapping at another of the bugs that was biting her arm. She knew she'd have welts all over, but really, there was nothing they could do but suffer them.

They passed by the barracks where the men were having their own celebration, and Mel asked Peter to make sure that they shut things down by midnight, so everyone was able to work the next day. Alinta knew that Mel didn't approve of the heavy drinking some of the men participated in. Alinta also didn't like to see anyone staggering about, and she followed Mel's lead on how she felt about it. She knew Mel would fire any man who didn't do his share of work, instead indulging in the drink too heavily.

CHAPTER SEVEN

Alinta was thrilled when Mel took a crew, including several aboriginal men, down the track with the men she had hired to build fences. Mel hadn't been surprised when Alinta saddled up her own horse and packed a bag for herself and Ainia. Alinta didn't want to stay in the house, which was full of furniture now. Mostly, she didn't understand what the furniture was for, and she had no idea where Mel wanted it to go. She knew Mel was pleased with everything that had arrived and was reluctant to go out to the folds to show these men where to work, but she had no choice. They were here now and would have to start the work she contracted with them to do.

Alinta certainly didn't care or understand about setting up of the house, but she knew it was important to Mel. While she could have helped the maid who arrived, she didn't really know what to do with

these odd things. They didn't make sense to her. She did appreciate the warm house and the beautiful windows that showcased their Outback, but she preferred being out of doors. She loved that she was riding a horse with Ainia on the saddle before her and seeing more of her beloved Outback. She was developing a sense of ownership to the land that she had never felt before. She thought of how Mel said she was *taming* the land. She laughed at this, knowing no one owned the land or tamed it. Rather, the land owned *you*, and you simply conformed to its whims. Even the great house on the hill might someday be taken away by the winds that came with the winter rains.

Alinta had been fascinated by one of Mel's latest acquisitions. It was an animal she called a cat. The cat had stunk, so Mel washed it. It had traveled far to come to them, and it was pregnant and due to give birth any day. The cat was like no animal Alinta had ever seen before. It wasn't like a dingo and was considerably smaller. It had stunk because of the box it traveled in and the care the men had taken in making sure it arrived on the station. Mel explained that its mate had disappeared on the long trip out to the station. Mel seemed to like the fierce animal, and Alinta watched it avidly. She too was reluctant to leave it as they headed down the track.

They camped at the second fold that first night. It was the third fold she and Mel had built. The stockman drew Mel's attention to an outcropping of rocks. Alinta had pointed out long ago that it contained ancient drawings. Both women felt the spirits that roamed this area, and they could see that others who traveled with them to look at the drawings were also affected, becoming uneasy and looking around.

Mel was upset that the stockman was requesting he be provided with dynamite to blast the outcropping.

"Does it interfere with the sheep eating grass around there?" Mel countered, lifting an eyebrow.

"No, but I thought you might want it…gone?" he hesitated, unsure what the owner meant. The outcropping gave him the willies.

"No, leave it. The aboriginal people, who have roamed this land forever might consider it sacred. I have no problem with it remaining. They are welcome to it, and it is theirs for all time. Leave it alone," she instructed him again, looking at him intensely to convey how important it was to her too. Blast it, indeed! "I'd rather you hunted dingoes than worrying about some drawings that people put on some rocks long ago."

"I've been hunting!" he protested immediately.

"Yes, but there are always more dingoes; there always seems to be more," she sighed, which was true.

Alinta could have told her why the dingoes were always around. Their numbers were increasing because of an abundance of food. With sheep coming into their territory, they would hunt the vulnerable animals. Alinta watched as Mel discussed the dingo problem with her men, instructing the stockmen at the various folds to clear some of the trees and remove extra brush that had sprung up since they had built the fold. "It'll give fewer hiding places for dingoes and other scavengers. We want grass, not brush." The men understood and nodded.

Alinta watched as Mel had the men begin building fences at what would become the southern and western corners of their station. Farther west was more desert, and Alinta knew that somewhere out there her people had their range. She was no longer sure exactly where it was, and she sighed, wondering what had happened to her mother, father, and brother. Eventually, she let go of those thoughts too. They

were in the past, but she wished she could show her family to Ainia. How her mother would have loved the sturdy, little girl.

Mel showed Alinta how a gate could be constructed in the fence they were putting up, which was the same combination of deadfalls, brush, and split rails they had used to make the folds. They simply lowered some of the poles to let a cart, horse, or wagon through, then put them back up. It wasn't fancy, but it was useful. She explained that she didn't want to infringe on Twin Station's land, and the domed hills were a good boundary for their own station.

They headed north after the men got going on the fence line that would enclose that first paddock. They were chopping down trees and brush and building it like the many folds they had constructed. Split rail seemed to spring up along the line rapidly as the many men worked. Mel and Alinta put up markers indicating where the fence should go as they traveled on their way north. Mel mentioned how much more arid it was in this section of the station, and Alinta nodded. She was enjoying the time alone with her husband and daughter. The three of them quietly rode along exploring and putting up markers that indicated where Mel wanted her station to end. Alinta hadn't been this happy in a long time. They sat together at night with the fire crackling merrily. They ensured the fire was not so large that it impeded their view of the night sky, which seemed endless, beautiful, and all theirs. They murmured quietly, so they didn't intrude on the feel of the night upon them as they lay there. They watched Ainia toddle about importantly. She was picking up sticks and stones and beginning to use nonsense words, which was a delight for both parents. Eventually, they had to go back, but this little trip invigorated them. Slowly, they headed back, still marking the western, desert-like border in places before they arrived approximately even with where the home paddock lay by Mel's estimate. She wasn't sure if the creek that petered out in the desert here was the same creek that ran through the home paddock, and they followed it quite a ways until a cliff impeded their ability to continue. They couldn't really go around, and Mel didn't want to climb it with Ainia along, so they backtracked until they found the track and headed for home. Alinta had really enjoyed the trip and regretted having to return home to work, but she was strangely thrilled to see the home paddock come into view as they rode up the hill.

Alinta could see how thrilled Mel was to find that furniture had been placed about the house. The new maid, Betty Firth, smiled shyly at the praise Mel gave her. Alinta smiled in agreement with her mate as they looked at the furniture. Mel wanted some things moved, and the maid and Alinta helped her place them where they belonged as the house finally came to order.

Alinta watched the cat, which had given birth while they were away. Betty confided to Mel that she had burned the stinky crate, and Alinta smiled. She was used to earthy smells, but even she had noticed the odor, and Mel agreed it needed to go. The cat had settled in and was living in the kitchen now that there was a place for Mel and Alinta in the finished master bedroom. The cat was fascinating, its fur was soft, and the mewing babies were precious.

Ainia was fascinated, and Mel let her hold a kitten after cautioning her with, "Gentle now, be careful." The unsteady girl was seated on the floor of the kitchen, her legs out before her, and gently touching the

soft kitten. When it mewed, she looked up in wonderment. The mother cat looked to see if the kitten was in distress and then closed her eyes to slits of contentment as the other kittens suckled.

"Okay, let's give this baby back to its mama," Mel said after Ainia had petted it for a while. But it would prove to be harder than that to return the kitten. The little girl was not used to being told no, and finally, Alinta had to take the protesting toddler out of the room while Mel put the kitten to its mother's teat and left them alone.

"I been giving her a drop of cow's milk, if that's okay," Betty confessed, wondering if she had overstepped at all. Mel was a big man and intimidating to her.

"No, that's a good idea. We want those kittens to grow up strong and help around the place." Mel mused for a moment, thinking. "I better send for a tomcat in my next batch of supplies." She wondered what had happened to the father of these kittens on the trip out and if it would be a problem for anyone if he survived and showed up on their station.

Alinta helped Mel unpack books in the study. What she called a large desk also sat in the room. It was a pretty, dark red color. Mel placed the books on shelves that O'Grady had built and some of her men had sanded and stained. Alinta's fingers had touched the smooth wood many times as she marveled at the color. She went on about the other chores that needed doing, including getting Ainia to bed as Mel sat down to write letters.

"Come to bed?" she asked Mel later, and her husband looked up in surprise at the lateness of the hour.

"Time got away from me," she answered with a smile. Alinta wondered at the smile that deepened as Mel got up, blew out the desk lamp, and joined her wife to head upstairs to their bedroom. She had slept in a bed before at Twin Station but preferred the ground or even the floor of the kitchen that they had used for a while.

"Spring?" she asked when Mel explained that this mattress was different than the stuffed mattresses they had slept on at Twin Station.

"Yes, it's a piece of steel that they coil around, so it springs back if you bend it a little," she explained, trying to keep it simple since Alinta had nothing to compare it to her in experience. "I'll show you someday," she promised as she washed up in the porcelain bowl of the sink in their bathroom.

Alinta followed Mel's lead and washed up as well, wondering at the odd little smile her husband sported. She had no idea one of the letters Mel had received and responded to was from a Lady Worthington, a first love from Mel's past. Mel had compared Alinta to the high-born lady and found the love she felt for Alinta was nothing like the love she had felt for Abigail. Alinta was an earthy, primitive woman, and completely in tune with her surroundings. Abigail Worthington would never survive in the Outback.

As Alinta washed, she thought about something she had observed. She noticed that Mel seemed to want to make love to her more often when she washed up, and she eagerly anticipated more of that.

Mel began to undress, even removing the wraps that she used to bind her breasts.

Alinta asked, "Bath?" as her husband got naked. She understood that *husband* usually referred to a man, but Mel didn't want her accidentally referring to her as *wife* in front of others and had asked repeatedly that she use husband instead.

Mel had a beautiful body, and Alinta hoped the bath was a prelude to the lovemaking she anticipated. The feelings that Mel invoked in her young body were unlike anything she had experienced with anyone else. She hadn't even known these feelings existed in her body. The one time that Mel had used her tongue between the primitive woman's legs, Alinta had been confused at first, and then, she relaxed and experienced an ecstasy she hadn't known existed. She'd nearly pulled out Mel's hair as she grasped the back of her head in her spasms. Mel had grinned, wiped the moisture from around her mouth, and then lain on the smaller woman, making her feel surrounded not only by Mel's bulk but also by her love as she warmed the other woman's body with her own.

"Yes, would you like to join me?" Mel asked, looking at her wife speculatively and wondering if she would be brave enough.

Alinta looked up, wondering briefly if Mel was planning on drowning her in that tub. She'd had those same thoughts back when her wife insisted Alinta bathe in the creek long ago. The thought of voluntarily immersing her whole body in water had been repugnant to her. Alinta was used to normal human smells, sweat, and dust on her body, which helped ward off the constant flies and other bugs in the Outback. She had hated the feel of her skin when it was clean. It had felt vulnerable and raw, and she noticed that the bugs certainly liked it. That Mel liked it too was soon apparent, and she accommodated her, especially once they became intimate. It was especially nice to be able to clean away the blood when her time was upon her, and Mel had shown her how to use the rags. Since they were soon cycling together, it was a good cover for Mel that Alinta could wash their rags together. She saw the mischievous grin on her husband's face and was up to the challenge as she removed her man's shirt that looked like a dress on her small frame. She then removed the boots Mel had had shipped in for her, finding them difficult to wear at first and now liking that they protected her feet from stones and snakes. She'd been impressed that Mel's knee-high boots had kept her from being bitten by the death adder. It was another white man thing she could admire.

Mel liked knowing that Alinta didn't wear anything under her clothes...no corsets, no petticoats...nothing. In winter, she had condescended to wear summer underwear, but she hated the flap out the back that allowed her to sit and make her stream, having wetted the material more than once before the toilets in the house were installed. Alinta liked the swirling water that took away the waste, finding the toilets fascinating.

As the hot coming from the water reservoir behind the stove downstairs filled the tub, Mel smiled in anticipation. She liked the idea of sitting in the tub for a while with Alinta and maybe washing her hair. Although she had given the woman her brush, Alinta rarely used it on her wild tresses. Mel liked the wildness of her wife's hair. Her own hair was short, and she kept it that way deliberately, so she only needed a comb to keep it under control. Mel stepped gingerly into the hot water, turning the cold water on a little stronger until it was more of an even warm temperature so as not to burn her wife's skin. She finally turned off the tap and sat back. Her bulk spread out the water, so less had been needed to fill the tub.

Alinta stepped into the tub in front of Mel. She was not used to hot water at all, although there were some hot springs her father once took them to. The hunting was poor in that area and it smelled oddly, so they didn't stay there long. Now, this ability to draw hot water from a faucet, a word that had been hard for her to learn, amazed her. Alinta sat back against Mel, who lifted one of her own legs and put it on the side of the tub to make room. She liked this feeling of skin on skin.

Mel loved touching the muscular body of her young wife. She was amazed that there was no sign the woman had ever been pregnant except for a tiny pucker in her midriff. Mel's soapy hands went up and down the woman's arms, feeling the tender skin.

Alinta had never imagined that the caress of another human being could make her feel the way Mel made her feel. She desired her husband, and her arousal was almost instantaneous as they lay in the warm bath together and touched. She held off though, wondering what Mel would do and enjoying her ministrations.

Alinta had never imagined how it would feel to have someone massage her scalp; there was no word for *massage* in her native language. No one had ever touched her as Mel did, and she loved the fingers that probed gently but tried not to think about the soap that she worked into her hair. Used to seeing matted hair on the stockmen and aboriginal people, who never brushed out their hair, she would have been fine with that. Mel had introduced her to brushing, and while she didn't brush her hair every day, it was brushed often enough that the oils it contained came out and made it look lovely. Mel had cut her hair off just below her shoulder blades, so it was easier for her to handle, and she enjoyed it since she had never thought of doing this before. Mel also admitted to enjoying running her fingers through

Alinta's hair, missing the days when she had long hair and reminded of the feminine part of her that was long lost.

Gently, Mel cleansed her wife's hair and moved down from there to her lovely shoulders that were so soft and were no longer dark brown as she had seen them when her wife wore less. She continued under her arms, washing the long hair there and wondering why this too was different from her own. She had discovered that Alinta was ticklish when she washed down her sides and her short legs. Finally, she began to wash between her wife's legs. There was always the temptation to play with the curls that grew there, but she made sure to wash between the folds, anticipating kissing them later, her mouth watering at the thought of tasting Alinta. She even washed her crack, up and down and then back to the front, making sure she didn't miss any fold or leave behind any soap residue.

Alinta moaned when Mel *accidentally* touched the nub of flesh she hadn't known was there until her husband taught her. She wanted this woman and turned in the tub, intending to wash her too. Mel's eyes enthralled her, surprising her with their intensity as she began to wash her, returning the favor. She was so white, the tan on her face ending at the collar where her button-down shirts began. Alinta was amazed to see her arm against this white skin and how it looked so dark.

Mel watched through slitted eyes, enjoying the caresses with the washcloth as the water in the tub cooled. They took a long time in the tub, but she didn't mind. Her wife was touching her breasts, seeming to enjoy tweaking them, and they stood up not only from the cold but also from her knowing touch. Mel smiled as she saw the teasing smile forming around her wife's mouth; she knew exactly what she was doing to her. Alinta moved on to Mel's torso, moving inexorably down

to her legs and then between them. Mel couldn't help gasping at the feel of Alinta's hand between her legs. She desperately wanted to feel that touch. Teaching Alinta what pleased her had been one of the best things about being married to her. She had waited for her for so long—first, for her to give birth to their daughter and then, for them to have the privacy she wanted—and she was pleased with how willing a lover Alinta had become. They had turned a terrible incident for the young woman into a pleasure that she now eagerly participated in, initiating their lovemaking on more than one occasion.

She didn't stop at the washing this time. She was wondering if the moans coming from Mel's mouth meant she could make her husband come undone. She dropped the washcloth, rubbing between the folds, and Mel spread her legs as wide as the tub allowed giving Alinta access as she played. Alinta lifted one leg, putting it along her own hip in order to get closer, her fingers slipping inside her husband as she watched her reaction.

Mel's head fell back, and her other foot reached out, stretching as the sensations began to build and her body began to tense. Unknowingly, she hit the plug in the tub, and it began to drain. She was completely unaware of the lack of water as Alinta began to work her body, leaning down over her husband's body to suckle and tease at the erect nipples that begged for attention. This had startled Alinta at first. She had thought nipples were only for feeding babies. She learned that pleasure and pain could be had from this, and she had greatly enjoyed the pleasure, pleased that Mel was willing to give her plenty of it. For now, Mel wouldn't suckle at Alinta's nipples. She had said many times that the milk was for their daughter, and it was precious to her.

As Alinta's hand fell into rhythm—in and out, in and out—her fingers slipped in the wetness Mel was generating. She watched, looking up from where her mouth was working the woman's nipple when she heard Mel's breath catching. Slowly, she played at the larger woman's body and was pleased when her thumb hit the flesh that stood up slightly from the fold. It was merely a bump, but that bump was so tender and sensitive that Mel was soon thrashing in the tub. The water was almost all gone from the tub as she came and came again, her body tense, then supine, then tense again. Her toes curled as she gasped out a final orgasm, her mouth set stubbornly closed, so her moans wouldn't echo in the bathroom's confines.

Mel slowly opened her eyes. She had not expected her wife's tender touch to turn so erotic. She smiled as Alinta rose from where she lay on her body, giving her warmth in the aftermath of their lovemaking.

"That was…unexpected," Mel murmured softly, feeling emotions she couldn't put into words as she gazed down into the earthy woman's face. Her hands wrapped around the slender woman, holding her to her own bulk.

Alinta looked at her husband earnestly. "Okay?" she asked. That one word said so much, telling Mel that Alinta worried she had done something wrong.

Mel cupped her wife's face, pulling her up her body as she did so and reaching to kiss her passionately. She was wishing she could turn over in the confines of the tub. She wanted to cover her wife's body with her own, press down, and take her. Instead, she kissed her passionately, telling her without words that she was more than okay. Slowly, she opened her mouth and her tongue came into play.

Teaching Alinta how to kiss using her tongue had been fun. She was such an avid apprentice that now her kisses were an intoxicant that could be Mel's undoing once again if she wasn't careful. "Let's go to bed," she murmured, intending to take her wife in their bed again, perhaps more than once. Her body was already feeling aroused again as Alinta got up and smiled cheekily, carefully getting out of the slippery tub. When Mel got up, the water that had built up behind her bulk suddenly sloshed towards the drain. She cupped some of it to wash her privates once more before getting out of the tub, her wife handing her a towel. Mel only superficially dried her body before capturing the wild woman in her arms and kissing her again, then lifting her up and carrying her to their bed.

CHAPTER EIGHT

Mel slept well, but she heard Ainia during the night. She was surprised that Alinta hadn't heard the baby. Alinta normally had the senses of a wild animal, and only the fact that Mel knew she had exhausted her lover in their love play kept her from becoming concerned that she didn't awaken at their daughter's cries. Mel wrapped her robe tightly around her. She was pleased with this robe that had come from Sydney. It fit her well and was made of a material that didn't cling to her frame, which allowed her to wear it without wrapping her breasts. She tied it off as she went to get their daughter, finding her crying in the room they had set up especially for their baby. There was a matching crib in their room as Mel had had O'Grady make two of them, but she was grateful the little girl hadn't been in their room the previous night. She shushed Ainia, changed her, and washed her lightly, so the urine that had cooled her and awoken her didn't remain on her skin. She changed Ainia's clothes and wrapped her in a blanket, but the poor little girl was still restless, and Mel knew this meant she was hungry. Mel was going to have to wake Alinta; she was sorry that she couldn't feed their daughter.

As she walked into their bedroom, closing and locking the door behind her, she looked at Alinta in the light of the lamp she had left turned down low on the table beside their bed. The serene look on her wife's face made her smile about the vigorous lovemaking they had participated in earlier. Alinta looked calm and peaceful, and if she felt as good as Mel, she needed to sleep. Ainia squirmed, reminding her that the baby needed to be fed. Alinta was still naked, and Mel wondered if she could manage to feed their daughter without waking the woman. She slowly crawled into their bed, angling the baby at her wife's exposed and obviously full breast. The child latched on with an enthusiasm that made Mel cringe. That had to hurt, but her wife never flinched. Instead, her breathing changed, and she slowly woke up, looking down at the baby in surprise, then back up at Mel. She smiled slowly as she snuggled the baby closer to her. Her hand reached out, caressing Mel's arm in remembrance of their earlier intimacy. Mel loved this moment so much, she could have cried, and she hoped she would remember it forever. She watched as the baby suckled, and when she was finished with the one breast, Alinta made a move to sit up, but Mel stopped her.

Taking the baby, she whispered, "Roll over and scoot onto this side," she indicated where she was getting off the bed. She carried Ainia around the bed and got back into bed, scenting the wet spot that had dried with her wife's amour. They repeated the position, tucking the baby in against Alinta again. The baby wasn't as hungry anymore, content with the nearly full stomach from the first breast. She was soon dozing off while occasionally sucking. Mel picked Ainia up and put her against her shoulder, patting her back gently to help get the bubbles up. As she looked around the large master bedroom, she realized something was missing. They needed a rocking chair, and she made a mental note to write for that in her next letter to Saunders' wife, requesting one for *someone* on the station, who had a baby. She had to be careful not to mention her wife to Saunders, his wife, or anyone else in Sydney who had known Melissa Lawrence.

Finally, the baby was burped and fell asleep again, content for a while. Mel picked her up and put her in the crib, gently laying her, so if she spit up it wouldn't choke her. It had taken several explanations before Alinta stopped bringing the baby into their bed, even when they laid on the floor. Mel explained that sometimes people rolled over in their sleep and squashed the baby, and she had finally convinced the inexperienced mother to keep their daughter nearby in a box, so she wouldn't roll anywhere, especially as she got older.

Alinta had never known a man to take care of a baby. She knew that Mel was not physically a man, but even the male spirit in her seemed to know how to take care of the baby. The men of her people were more interested in boy children but only when they reached a certain age and were out of swaddling clothes. Alinta was pleased that Mel thought of the baby as theirs.

Living in the desert, there hadn't been much clothing of any kind. The women preferred to hold the baby out in front of them when the baby pooped or peed as they strode along, pulling on leaves to wipe the baby and keep going, never stopping for these duties. They were

natural processes, and the women didn't give them another thought. White men and women seemed more concerned about their modesty. Mel returned to their bed, discarding her robe and glancing to see that the lock was engaged on their bedroom door before turning down the lamp, getting into bed with Alinta, and curling up against her frame. She thought of making love to her wife again but knew they had too much work to do the next day and couldn't afford to be that tired.

Mel woke slowly that morning, sensing even before she reached out that Alinta was gone from their bed. She was a lot quieter than Mel could ever hope to be. She lay there a moment, realizing that the birds tweeting their morning calls were a lot louder than her wife would be. She also realized Alinta had taken Ainia with her. When she finally got up, she saw that their clothes had been scooped up to be washed. She reached for a clean wrap to bind her breasts and began to pull on a shirt, pants, socks, and then her boots. Using her comb, she ran it through her hair for form's sake. Here in the house, she didn't shave it very often, allowing it to grow longer. Satisfied with her morning ritual, she used the bathroom and saw that Alinta had hung up their towels and opened a window to prevent mustiness in the enclosed room. The mosquito netting on the windows was a godsend, protecting against the bugs that would have swarmed into the house.

Mel headed downstairs to a hearty breakfast, pleased that her wife and the maid had it hot and ready for her. She ate well and went outside, watching the sun rising in the east and feeling quite pleased

with her life. She had everything she never knew she always wanted, and life was good. Alinta joined her.

"What do today?" she asked.

"What are we going to do today?" Mel parroted, correcting Alinta unconsciously as she tried to teach her wife better English. "Today, we are going to start building some bridges."

"Bridges?" Alinta asked, unfamiliar with the word.

"Yes, bridges. We need a couple bridges over the creek when the rains come, so we can still get over to the paddocks we are building."

Peter Winston, coming up to the house for his daily instructions, caught that last statement and smiled. "Want me to gather some men and get started?"

"Yes, and we will need to make the bridges the shape of an arch. If anyone knows how to do that, they should speak up; otherwise, we are going to have to learn by trial and error," Mel said with a smile as she looked down on her head stockman. She walked down off her porch and nearly tripped on a puppy that had escaped the barn. "We also need kennels for these little guys," she said, scooping up the young dog. Just then, one of the bitches came trotting from the barn. Hearing her pup's cry as Mel scooped him up, she turned it into a run. Mel put the pup back down before her, and the dog thoroughly sniffed the pup before picking it up by the scruff of its neck. The pup went totally limp, and the mother trotted back towards the barn where a bed was made up in one of the stalls for her and her mischievous pups.

Peter laughed as Mel started describing what she wanted. She was followed by Alinta, who veered off and headed for the chicken coop to collect eggs with their little girl. Mel was feeling expansive today, and her hands gestured enthusiastically as she elaborated on her ideas.

After dinner, Mel would sit down, relax, and write letters. Sometimes, Alinta practiced the letters and writing that Mel showed her while proudly complimenting her as she learned. She had a brilliant mind and only had to be told or shown once before she grasped new things. It was implementing what she learned that was sometimes hard and had to be repeated or corrected a few times. Still, once Alinta had it, she proudly showed off her writing, reading, and speaking skills.

CHAPTER NINE

It was about a week later that several men came riding in hell bent for leather and gathering help to fight a fire in one of Twin Station's northern paddocks. Alinta watched as Mel took a dozen men with her down the track, rushing to help fight the fire. She left word that anyone that could be spared was to head to the fire to help.

Alinta worried while Mel was gone with her men, but there was nothing she could do. She could faintly see the smoke on the horizon, but it was so far away that it looked like a mere wisp of a cloud. The heat shimmered as she gazed frequently towards the track and out over the land, looking towards where the fire fighters would return along this path. Holding Ainia, she glanced around at those left at the home paddock. They were busily going about their duties, and she noticed they too glanced frequently towards the track, wondering when the others would return or if they would receive word.

Mel and the men who had gone to fight the fire returned several days later, dusty and very dirty. The men either took advantage of the stopped-up creek and the pond it had made or headed for the bathhouse connected to the barracks. Two of them lived in the married stockmen's homes and had their own bathtubs, and Mel returned to the station house to immerse herself in the tub in their bathroom off the master bedroom. Alinta could understand her enjoyment of the tub. She had learned how delightful sharing a tub with her husband could be. She now kept herself very clean, using it because she knew her husband liked her cleanliness, and she appreciated the benefits she received in return.

"I swear, having that metal on the roof makes it hotter in the barns and sheds," Mel worried as the heat continued to intensify.

Alinta listened to her husband and glanced at the valuable metal that had been used throughout their building process. She thought her husband must be very rich to be able to afford these sheets of the corrugated iron that had been painted green and placed on the various buildings. It looked attractive and shed rain very well, but the Aborigine, whose father had impressed upon her the value of this white man's stone, couldn't help but wonder at her husband's complaint about so valuable a commodity. The heat would always be there—it always had been—and all they could do was wait for the weather to change and the rains to come. The sandstorms that came blasted against the buildings, and Mel reduced Alinta's chores, taking on the egg gathering in the poultry pens, so her wife wouldn't have to be out in the storms. Alinta was amused since no one had ever worried about such things where she was concerned before.

They found that going down into the hidden valley sometimes gave them a little relief from the horrible, hot winds. The dust, which still reached this valley, seemed to come down at an angle and left the beginning of the valley free of the choking mess, making it marginally cooler, especially in the early mornings and late evenings.

The dust built up everywhere, slipping through every crack and crevice. The house was constantly being bombarded, and their maid, Betty, dusted constantly. The windows and doors were kept closed, but that created a stifling atmosphere. Mel had Alinta take Ainia down into the cellars to play, so the child could keep cool. Betty had her sleeping quarters there, and there were other rooms set up and waiting for additional employees someday. Mel eventually placed a mattress on the floor, and she, Alinta, and Ainia slept down in the coolness, so they could breathe in the stifling heat.

Alinta watched as the boy Mel had staying in the house during the day trod up to the cupola at the top of the house to watch through the dry heat for signs of smoke from either dry lightning that had started the fire on Twin Station or other natural causes. A fire in the heat at this time of year could be devastating. By having the boy stationed up there, they were able to stop a small lightning strike in one of the paddocks.

The clouds rolled in but only brought lightning that was striking the earth from time to time and starting fires. The clouds also brought

hope of rain, but instead, remained miles away, deceptive in their innocence.

Alinta made sure Willie, the boy watching for signs of smoke, was fed and took breaks from the stifling heat at the top of the house. Her own eyesight, better than anyone's on the station, could take in things that the whites didn't even notice as she took a turn while Willie was down in the kitchen eating tiffin.

Alinta enjoyed playing with the kittens and teaching Ainia to be gentle with the soft creatures as they cavorted in the shade of the porch. Alinta knew that Mel felt these animals were important to the station and would help keep down the rodents that were drawn by what they thought were easy meals and convenient places to live and breed in the various buildings.

Mel returned from fighting a small, dry lightning-induced fire and was pleased to see her wife and daughter on the porch. She was greeted by Willie too, who had some news to import but was held off by Mel's need to bathe.

"Pa!" Ainia greeted her, pleased to see the big man as she got off her horse, handing it off to one of the other boys.

"Hang on there, darling," Mel warned, putting up her hands, her grubby clothing something she didn't want to taint her daughter. Alinta stopped the toddler from rushing Mel and laughed as the child strenuously objected.

"You get any tiffin?" Mel asked Willie, using the word Australians used for supper or dinner, depending on the time of day.

"Yes, sir. Missus Lawrence makes sure I get me grub twice a day," he assured her.

Mel smiled. She still loved hearing that missus part. "That's good. I'm going up to bathe," she announced to both Alinta and Willie. "You better get back to watching for smoke and dust," she told him and watched as he scampered off.

"You okay?" Alinta asked, glancing at the fatigue she could see on her husband's face.

"I'm good. Could use some water," she admitted as she headed inside. "Anything wrong with the well?" she stopped to ask, looking at her wife questioningly.

"Down some," she admitted. "Take bath," Alinta ordered with a grin, her white teeth looking very bright against her lips.

Mel returned the smile before nodding and heading inside to the stairs. After a good soak in the bath, washing off the dust and debris of fighting the small fire, and putting on clean clothes, she felt loads better. She went to eat in the kitchen, pleased to talk to Betty as she arranged for additional people to help in the house before she joined Alinta on the wide porch with their daughter. She swung Ainia around, delighting in her squeals of laughter.

"How have you been, luv?" she asked her wife, pleased to have this time alone if only for a few minutes.

"Hot," Alinta understated, fanning herself as she sat on the shady porch in one of the chairs the men had made. There wasn't a breath of fresh air, and she'd take Ainia inside soon to get out of the heat even though the house was stifling too. The basement was still marginally cooler, and it would be better to take her down there.

Mel chuckled but agreed with her wife, glancing towards the west and hoping that the clouds she saw there were rain clouds and not just building up to bring more dry storms.

"So, I sees this man on the track, but when he sees riders from the station he goes into the brush and hides. I don' see 'im for a while and then he is closer. I think he went along the track but in the brush out of sight."

"Did he come up to the paddocks? Find Peter to get hired on?" Mel asked Willie, who was reporting what he had seen. Alinta listened, not understanding every word, but she had learned this habit a while ago and would ask Mel later about those words she needed an explanation for.

"No, sir. I ain't seen him again at all. Then later, I thought I caught a glimpse, but he went back into the brush."

Mel frowned at that. Many of the swagmen were eccentric, and perhaps, he was just taking his time about making an appearance…scoping out Lawrence Station and the home paddock before asking for rations. She looked down towards the track that Willie had indicated as the sun was setting. The heat hadn't lessened, and there were shimmers of heat as she gazed out on the horizon. "Okay, Willie, you better head home for the day or your ma is going to think you live here," she teased. She smiled as the boy ran off down the hill for the stockmen's houses along the creek. She glanced to where men were working around the barns and sheds, shoveling sand from inside them or around them. Since it was marginally cooler with the sun setting, she had told the men to work only during the morning and evening hours, avoiding anyone becoming ill in the hot afternoon sun.

Alinta was just about to ask something to clarify what Willie had said when Peter, the head stockman, walked up to talk to Mel. "We better get some rain soon or sheep will be dying off."

"Anyone hear from the folds?" she asked, tired from her own day and about ready to head in to bed. She glanced at Alinta before turning her attention back to the man.

"Nothing we weren't expecting; graze is down everywhere. One of the men reported food missing, but he may have been mistaken."

"Food disappeared from his hut while he was out with the sheep?" Mel asked.

Peter nodded. "I think he just wanted more than his fair share of rations," he chuckled, and Mel smiled. Thinking this over, Mel suddenly asked, "Was it one of the folds on the way towards the track to Wilcannia?"

"Aye, it was. Something important about that?"

Mel told Peter about the man that Willie had spotted with the telescope. "He may just be checking us out before approaching, but maybe he helped himself to some extra supplies while the stockman was out with the sheep?"

Peter nodded, and he too looked a little concerned. With no further instructions forthcoming, he bid Mel good night and headed back to the barracks. He was one of the stockmen who was sending for his wife and children now that he had the lay of the land out here on the station. With the position of head stockman, he now wanted his family with him. It would be safest if his wife and children traveled with the supply carts that would be coming after the rainy season. Mel had written the letter for him since he didn't know how to write, but the arrangements were made, and he was looking forward to seeing his family again.

The next day, they were all pulled from their beds as Willie pointed a finger at the smoke that was starting to the southwest. They rushed with tools in the carts, many of the men climbing aboard to help put the fire out before it could really get started.

"This weren't no natural fire," Peter pointed out to Mel as they finished the clean-up. The fire had only burned a couple of acres, but it could have been much worse, and they all knew it. It was a good thing Will had spotted it, and they'd been prepared with the cart full of tools.

"You mean it was deliberately set?" Mel asked, concerned.

Peter showed her where the fire had started near a campfire that had been left to burn with no ring of stones, which most people would know to lay.

"Who would do this?" Mel asked, alarmed.

"Someone who wants to burn you out?" Peter asked, wondering at the strange man they had spoken of the night before. "I met an odd character a couple months back on the track..." he began and told her about the swagman, who had been angry to find out Mel's identity as the owner of the station.

"Wonder who that could be?" Mel asked.

"I don't know, but he seemed like an odd one. I didn't tell you about him because I assumed that was the end of it when he disappeared into the brush."

"I wonder if it's the same man that Willie spotted." She was pondering who would have such a grudge against her that they would deliberately start a fire, someone that would jeopardize not only her station but the many people working for her, their livelihoods, and the livestock. "See if you can track who did this, Peter. Ask some of the Aborigines if any of them are trackers. I want to know who did this."

Peter nodded and went to his horse to start casting about.

Alinta was concerned when Mel related all this to her. She hated having to stay at the house with Ainia, but she understood that she had to look after their small daughter.

CHAPTER TEN

They were all relieved when the threat of fires was lessoned somewhat the next week as the clouds sent them some badly needed rain. Unfortunately, it wasn't enough, and it was too early for the drenching downpours they would get with the rainy season. Mel pointed out that they seemed to get a little more rain in the southern pastures this time.

As they worked together in the garden one day, they were both surprised to see Carmen and Fabiola coming up the track. Mel was repairing the paddle on the wheel that pulled water into the garden. The water levels were so low that every bit of moisture they could get was necessary to keep the plants alive. Alinta was gathering vegetables and looked up, spotting their guests sooner than anyone else. She shaded her eyes despite the stockman's hat she was wearing.

"Well, hello there. Out pleasure riding on this fine day?" Mel teasingly asked their guests.

"Believe me, I wouldn't have made that ride just for pleasure," Fabiola told her as she got down from her horse. It was one of Carmen's fine blacks, and Mel admired it. It looked proud and strong even after that long ride.

"We have a present for you and wanted to discuss something," Carmen said as she came forward pulling a young stallion that was a fine imitation of her stallion, Dancer.

"*Oh, Carmen,*" Mel said reverently, taking the rope she offered with pleasure. Mel immediately let the young stallion sniff her and get used to her scent, and then she reached up to pet the fine, young beast. Alinta watched her husband's genuine pleasure over the beast. She could see it was a superior animal and thought she understood Mel's joy. She'd learned to really admire these beasts of burden and could see that Carmen's horses, which she knew her husband venerated, were superior to most of the animals they had in their own herd.

Carmen smiled, pleased with her friend's reaction. Mel had paid for this horse a couple years ago as they shared their long trip to the Outback. "Yes, I haven't named him, but the vaqueros are calling him El Diablo." She waited to see if Mel knew what that meant.

"The Devil?" Mel asked and started laughing at Carmen's nod. Alinta was pleased to have another word to add to her vocabulary. She heard both the Spanish word and Mel's English version. Mel had once told her a scary story of the devil, and she glanced at the young, black horse in speculation.

Fabiola was relieved to be rid of this young horse in more ways than one. This youngster was causing trouble in their home paddocks and had to be kept well away from Dancer, who already sensed a competitor for his harem of mares. Already, they had had to rebuild two of the fine, new stalls that O'Grady had built for them because of Dancer's temper tantrums while trying to get at this young buck. It was for that reason and others that they had decided to make this trip.

Mel reverently starting petting and patting the horse, loving his conformation and seeing his proud head come up to look around after he had carefully sniffed her. She examined him thoroughly and smiled at the bargain she had made so long ago. As a two-year-old, she might not be able to breed him– Just then, Carmen interrupted her train of thought.

"He is game, he is," she told her. "I'm not so sure he hasn't already covered one or two of my mares, and I thought it was time to bring him home." She blushed slightly at the indelicate subject, but she was a horse rancher in part and breeding was natural.

"I'm glad you did," Mel told her as she gazed at the fine specimen. Even after traveling all this way from Twin Station he looked fresh and willing to go on for miles. A two-year-old already covering mares? She shook her head. The stallion she had gotten with her herd of mares was not going to be happy. "Let's get him into his own stall, and you can tell me why you really made this long trip. A groom could have brought this happy boy," she crooned to the horse, trying to befriend him. He was eyeing her and switching his tail, not only at the flies that plagued them all.

"Hello, Alinta," Carmen said, giving the aboriginal woman a hug with one arm. She was pleased to see her. "Where's that precious daughter of yours?"

"She play in the mud," she said, pointing to where Ainia was playing happily in the dirt. "No, no, don't eat," she warned the toddler, going over to pick her up.

Ainia noticed the horse just then, the one obviously younger than the others. She looked at the strange women staring at her and went to put her filthy fingers in her mouth. Alinta stopped her, and Mel, who was watching, laughed.

"We keep her close with snakes and other things about."

"I had to hire another nurse to help Maria and Gabriella keep track of my children," Carmen lamented. "I think I need bridles on those boys."

Mel laughed as was expected, her attention now back on the young horse. "Come on up to the house, and we'll get you settled. You're staying the night, aren't you?"

"Yes, but only one night. We have to get back," Fabiola warned her, walking behind the large woman with her own horse.

"Alinta, do you want to ride on the horsey?" Carmen offered.

That was when Mel realized Carmen wasn't riding her beautiful stallion, Dancer. "Where is Dancer? Is he okay?"

"I had some of our men hold him back, so this young upstart, El Diablo, didn't start something. He has bad manners sometimes," she said, her delicious Hispanic accent making it sound intriguing. She gestured to the men that were inspecting the bridge Mel and her men had made at the beginning of the season. It was high and dry and looked ludicrous sitting there over the trickle that was now their creek.

Mel laughed again, pleased with the naughty, young stallion as she walked up the hill, her guests following her. Her wife followed the guests, holding tight to the dirty Ainia, who was clapping her muddy hands together causing even more of a mess. Alinta noticed the muddy handprints on her shirt but didn't mind because Ainia was happy.

Ainia was handed off to Betty once Alinta washed her up, and the little girl went down for a nap with almost no squawking. Mel fixed watered down rum for her guests, and they all sat on the porch of the house. The vaqueros that had accompanied their senora headed for the barracks and the hall.

"We have a problem," Fabiola began without any airs. "Someone is camping on our land and has left their campfire burning, which started a few fires. We've been unable to track him so far."

Mel exchanged a look with Alinta before she addressed her guests. "We had a suspicious fire too, same situation, they left a campfire burning. Peter went out with the Aborigines to track him but found nothing. He simply disappeared." She also told of the man that Willie had seen through the telescope.

"If he's been starting fires, he has to be stopped," Fabiola said passionately and angrily. At this moment, Mel could see the Aborigine in her features; she looked fierce and primitive.

"I agree, but one man alone could hide out there indefinitely," she pointed, gesturing to the rolling hills and gullies of the Outback.

"If he's lighting fires, we'll find him," Fabiola promised menacingly.

Mel had to agree. It was so beyond irresponsible that she was alarmed. It wasn't the miles of scorched land that it would cause that bothered her the most, it was the loss of life. Her men, these men who had come to work for her, depended on her for their livelihoods. They'd put down their lives to put out any fire on or off the station and had already demonstrated that in the two skirmishes they'd had.

It was nice to visit with the couple from Twin Station, but when inquiries about Harold's whereabouts were met with diverted conversations, Mel dropped the subject. She showed them the improvements that had been made since the last time they visited, and Fabiola talked her out of one of their kittens, whispering it was for Carmen's female cat that had been in heat many times with no relief since it had arrived on the station. The male she chose was a thin, gangling, black thing, but who knew the potential in the adolescent kitten. She rode off the next day with the kitten hanging out of her saddlebag, its small face looking out sorrowfully at its odd view of the world.

Mel was uneasy. If they had a maniac out there lighting fires, they all needed to be on high alert. She went down to the barracks and made an announcement in the hall about what the Twin Station owners had told her and added her own suspicions along with what Peter had told her about seeing the swagman. "I don't want Lawrence Station to be considered unfriendly, but until this man is caught or moves on, we need to be a little more cautious about swagmen or visitors." She knew visitors wouldn't be a problem since they rarely had them. Most were open and friendly, but they had to be cautious about this one that was hiding.

Alinta was uneasy. She could feel something in the air, and it felt like the heat waves that came in droves across the plains. She could sense something, and she didn't know what it was. It made Ainia upset whenever her mother tried to hold her as she could also sense something coming from her mother. Mel was the only one that could calm the toddler, but frequently, she was tired from hauling water to the stock. The creek was nearly dry, and they were all very worried. The

few scattered showers that had fallen weren't nearly enough. The moisture was quickly gobbled up by the parched land and the animals, and it evaporated into the hot air.

CHAPTER ELEVEN

The smoke of a fire was spotted by Willie, and he sounded the alarm. Mel kissed Alinta goodbye. They could both see by the size of the clouds that this fire was a big one. From the distance, she estimated it to be in the second paddock from the station. The men piled into the carts along with some of the women and the Aborigines. The fire was being carried rapidly along by the heat waves, creating its own winds and burning everything in its path.

Alinta watched as they rapidly left down the track, then she picked up Ainia and headed for the garden. Their work would continue despite the fire, and it was a good way to keep their minds off what their husbands were fighting. The other women joined her as they weeded and cultivated the plants, hauling up more water because the water level was so low in the creek that the water wheel wasn't working properly.

"I go fetch cold water from the house," Alinta offered, wiping her brow after they had been working for a few hours with the setting sun. Mel had told people not to work except first thing in the morning or in the evening when it was cooler, but it was still hot enough that they all sweated. The cool water from the house well sounded good, and the others agreed to watch Ainia for her while she fetched the water.

Alinta hadn't taken more than a few steps into the house when she was attacked. The man was angry and kept hissing things in her ear, but Alinta was so afraid she didn't hear them or understand them as she tried to fight him off. He hit her repeatedly, knocking her to the floor as she resisted. He finally hit her head on the wood of the floor, and everything was a daze after that for her. Betty found her there, and she began to wretch, not only from what had happened to her but also from the bruising around her neck that made it hard to breathe and swallow. Together, they got her upstairs to her bed where Betty left her. Alinta slowly took off her clothes and got into her nightgown, unwashed. After that she curled up in the bed. She had nightmares, and it caused her to sweat. She thrashed in her sleep and was only vaguely aware when Betty asked her about Ainia. She didn't respond, just lay there looking into nothingness and waiting to die. She was aware when Betty forced water through her parched lips and down her throat, but she didn't respond.

Later, Alinta became vaguely aware that it had started to rain, but for the most part she lay there and stared. Sometimes, she was lucid. Other times, she wasn't even aware of the passage of time. She wasn't even aware later that Mel was there.

"What's wrong, darling?" she asked tenderly, looking down at her wife. She had never seen the aboriginal woman ill even once in all the time she had known her. Even while pregnant and giving birth there was a hearty constitution to this woman.

Alinta barely looked at her husband, and when she finally focused in on the dirty figure of a man, she nearly recoiled.

"Alinta?" Mel asked, not understanding as her wife cringed from her touch. "Alinta, what's wrong?"

It was her voice that got through to the woman. Alinta blinked, seeing the woman she loved beneath the filth and not the manly figure Mel projected to the rest of the world. Her short hair was full of grime, and her face looked as dark as Alinta's skin.

"Mel? Mel?" she began to sob as she sat up and wrapped herself around the bigger woman, grateful to have her there.

"Shhh, shhh," Mel crooned, rocking her wife and petting her tangled hair. "What's the matter? Shhh, shhh." She tried, but it was a good twenty minutes before Alinta finally stopped sobbing and hiccupping. Mel got up and closed the door, locking it. She fished for a handkerchief in the dresser and handed it to her wife but only after she carefully wiped the tears from the woman's face. "Are you better?" she asked, worrying about what would cause her wife to cry like this. Alinta never cried. "What's wrong?" she asked next, seeing her wife was *not* better.

"Man…man…" Alinta hiccupped and cried a little more into the handkerchief, realizing some of the grime and dirt from Mel had gotten on her face and was now on the bed.

Mel could smell the sweat on her wife and worried that she had caught some tropical disease or something. There was no doctor out

here, and they did the best they could when someone was hurt. She didn't know what was wrong with the woman, and it was breaking her heart to hear her crying still; however, it was less than the earlier torrent. "Tell me slowly. It's okay," she said, trying to take her wife's hands in her own grimy hands. She wished she could wash, but she had to find out what was wrong with her wife, who was obviously distraught.

"Man, he come, he come," she said, unable to get out much before she started crying again, and then Mel noticed she looked ashamed.

"A man came to the house?" she asked, beginning to be afraid for her wife. It was then she noticed the fading finger marks on Alinta's neck. "What is that?" she asked, reaching to touch them below the nightgown her wife was wearing. That was another unusual thing...Alinta rarely wore the gowns Mel had bought for her, preferring to wear the men's long, dress-like shirts or go about naked in their bedroom.

Alinta flinched, but Mel's finger caught on the neck of the nightgown and pulled it away, revealing more fading bruises.

"Oh, my God," Mel exclaimed as she pulled the blankets back. She pulled up the gown and revealed even more bruising on her wife's body. "Are you like that all over?" she asked, horrified at the implications of what had happened while she was gone and wasn't there to protect her wife.

Alinta tried to cover herself, pulling her knees up under the gown and pulling it back down from where Mel had looked. She looked away, ashamed as she nodded and started sobbing, but it was less intense than before.

"Did he...? Did he...?" Mel began, but she knew. Even without asking her wife, she knew what the man had done. She gathered her wife close. At first, Alinta resisted, but Mel was so much stronger than she, and she needed the comfort of her *husband*, the only person who had ever been gentle and kind to her. Mel held her and rocked her, crying for what had happened to her young wife. Her own tears were dribbling down her face and into her wife's hair. They stayed like that for what seemed like hours, then Mel finally realized the passage of time by the shadows through the windows. As she gently lay her wife back on the bed, her relaxed body telling Mel that she was finally asleep, she wondered when the last time was that her wife had gotten any sleep. There were dark circles under her eyes, so it must have been quite a while. Mel covered her wife, noting the bruises on her arms and wondering at the man who had done this. She quietly got up and went into the bathroom, closing the door to keep the sound of the water from waking Alinta.

Mel cried some more as she undressed, and she cried as she bathed in the bathtub. She had dreamed of this soak on the ride back from the fire. She cried as she washed her hair and body, and she didn't linger as she had planned. Instead, she got right out of the tub when she was done. She had to wash the tub out to eliminate the line of filth from the edges. She washed the dirt down the drain and wished she could do the same to the man who had hurt her wife. As she was thinking these thoughts, she looked at the small bit of soot she had missed and realized that the fire had probably been purposely started to draw everyone away from the station, leaving only a few people to tend to the animals and leaving it open for the man to commit this savagery.

She closed her eyes for a moment, feeling the shame of being unable to save her wife from this.

"Mel?" Alinta called, and she rose from where she was washing the tub, grabbing her robe to wrap around her as she opened the door. "I think you leave me," the woman said as the shadows made her look small, thin, and very, very tragic.

Mel came to sit on the edge of the bed. "I'll never leave you," she told the woman, taking her into her arms. She could smell the sweat and fear on her wife. "Would you like a bath?" she asked carefully, wondering if Alinta was physically hurt beyond the bruising and not willing to ask her.

Alinta nodded, one short, quick jerk of her head, and Mel pulled the covers back again as she carried her wife into the bathroom and set her on her feet. "Wait here, and I'll get the water going," she said as she bent over to plug the tub and start filling it again. She gently turned back to her wife, who was looking down at her feet, and she lifted Alinta's head with her fingertips. "You are going to be okay," she said firmly, looking into those amazing, black eyes and feeling sorrowful.

Alinta nodded again. It was as though what Mel said was the way it was going to be. She allowed Mel to begin removing her gown, and Mel was hard-pressed to prevent herself from shouting out in anger when she saw the many bruises all over her wife's body. She wanted details, but at the same time, she knew her wife would probably never speak of this again. She helped Alinta into the tub and began washing her. Alinta closed her eyes as Mel massaged the soap into her hair, enjoying the familiar feel of her husband's fingers. Mel was careful not to touch the bruises. She wondered why some were still so vivid and looked very painful. She rinsed Alinta's hair and body and said, "Soak in here for a moment. I'm going to change the bed."

Alinta nodded, not saying anything as she lay there soaking in the warm water. Mel got up and went into the bedroom. Unlocking the door, she headed for the linen closet and got out new sheets and blankets for the bed. She went back in the bedroom and locked the door once again, quickly stripping the bed. She could see exactly where Alinta had lain for the last week; her body was outlined in sweat and dirt on the sheets. Her breasts must have leaked all over the sheets, and Mel wondered how Ainia had been fed while her mother lay in bed unresponsive, but she couldn't worry about their daughter now. After all, she had looked fine with Betty earlier.

Mel remade the bed, putting the pile of dirty bedclothes into the corner and picking her and Alinta's clothes up off the floor of the bathroom and putting them into the pile as well. She got herself dressed, including a new wrap, and she fished the other used wrap out of the wash, so Betty wouldn't see it. She'd wash it herself and hang it here in the privacy of the bedroom. Normally, Alinta took care of this for her. It was then she noted the blood on the dirty sheets. Knowing it wasn't Alinta's time of the month, she wanted to cry for what had been done to her wife.

Alinta was nearly asleep in the bathwater when Mel pulled the plug. Mel got her up and dried her with a bath sheet, wanting to wrap her in it as she stood there docilely. She dried her wife and dressed her in a man's shirt, hoping she would feel better in that. She tucked Alinta into the now clean bed, and when she would have left her, Alinta clasped onto her. "Shhh, shhh, don't cry," she told her. "I was just going to get you something to eat. Would you like to see Ainia?" she asked, wondering what she could do for her. She didn't know what else to do beyond what she was already doing.

Alinta shook her head. "No Ainia," she asserted stoutly as she lay back on the bed, her wet hair making the pillowcase damp.

"Hold on," Mel said, rising as she went to get another towel and grabbing the hairbrush off the dresser. She began to brush out her wife's tresses, something they had both greatly enjoyed in the past. It took a long time and reminded them both of happier times. The brushing and the bath exhausted Alinta. Mel put the towel down on the pillow and gently lay her wife's head against it. "You sleep some more," she nearly whispered. "I'm going to get something to eat, and then I'm going to bring you something to eat. I bet you haven't eaten in God knows how long. Am I right?"

Alinta, responding to the teasing note in Mel's voice, smiled wanly. Nodding once, she closed her eyes and sighed. She was relieved that Mel was there to take care of her and protect her.

Mel rose and put the brush back on the dresser. In stockinged feet she scooped the dirty clothes up in her arms and headed out of the bedroom, closing the door, so Ainia couldn't toddle in if she happened to be upstairs.

"Mr. Lawrence?" Betty asked when Mel came down with the laundry. The maid hurried to take it from her.

"Is there any food made?"

"Yes, sir, there's some soup on the stove," she said, wondering what had happened to make Mrs. Lawrence take to her bed. That wasn't like her in the least. Even when her time was upon her and the cramps were terrible, she didn't let anything stop her.

Mel dished up a large bowl of the soup, which was thick and more like a stew, and she sat down to eat it. She saw some biscuits and used them to dip into the filling meal. She knew this was one of Alinta's favorite meals, so when she finished her own bowl, she filled another and buttered some biscuits, then put them on a platter to take up to her wife.

Betty watched in worry, wondering what was going on. She'd taken the baby to one of the women who had stayed behind when the others left. She had a baby of her own, so she could help feed her. Ainia was with her now, but Betty knew the woman would expect her to come and get her soon.

Mel almost had to force Alinta to eat but talking to her about the horse named El Diablo helped to draw a smile from her. Except for the eyes, Alinta had teased that the horse was a bunyip in disguise. They'd both enjoyed the young horse's antics as he plagued their other stallion and the geldings. He also displayed himself to the mares, who seemed to watch the juvenile with humor. At two, he was fully developed; however, he'd be even more impressive when he was a three-year-old and an adult.

Alinta loved the butter-covered biscuits. Butter was something she had never eaten until Mel introduced it to her. Even the cheese that came out of the kegs didn't compare to the fresh cheese that one of the women knew how to make, and Alinta had avidly learned this skill from her. Not daring to say no to the owner's wife, they had taught her anything she wanted. As Alinta and Mel talked about anything but what was really bothering them, she gradually ate. She couldn't eat all the stew as her stomach had shrunk, but she was full and sleepy once again. Mel left her to take the tray downstairs.

"Is Mrs. Lawrence better?" Betty asked, worried.

"Pa!" Ainia called from where she had been messily eating at a special chair Mel had designed to tie her down. She was a wiggly creature, and it was a good thing she had been started on regular food. She mushed the small biscuit Betty had given her into the stew.

"You eat that," Mel told the little girl, who smiled and showed off the teeth she had developed as she tried to push the wet biscuit into her mouth and missed. Mel addressed Betty, "She's getting better." Her look flickered towards the upstairs, and the maid realized she was referring to the missus. "Thank you for taking care of them while I was gone." Mel tenderly finger combed Ainia's hair as the toddler continued to try stuffing the wet biscuit into her mouth. She was only succeeding occasionally, but she was having a lot of fun trying.

"I don't know what happened. We were all down at the garden, and the missus offered to come up and get some fresh well water for us to drink. When she didn't come back, I came looking for her and found her on the floor in the hall. She was so sick I barely got her upstairs. I found her in her nightgown the next morning, and she wouldn't eat or get out of 'er bed."

"When was this, Betty?" Mel asked as she used a spoon to feed the toddler some of the mashed-up vegetables in the stew. Ainia laughed and ate it gladly; she loved her food.

"A week ago, maybe two days after you all left for the fire."

Mel nodded. She certainly couldn't ask the maid for some of the more intimate details, not that she would know anything anyway. She was surprised the maid hadn't noticed the many bruises on her wife. "How did you all fare while we were gone?" she asked, seemingly innocently, as she fed Ainia. When the toddler had had enough to eat,

Mel washed her face, and she resisted the washcloth angrily. Mel had heard the maid relate enough mundane things that she realized the girl couldn't tell her anything, and no one had seen anything.

Mel cleaned Ainia up, gave her a bath in the sink, and then got her ready for bed. She read to her in her own room from one of the many children's books Mel had sent for and which she had read to both her wife and daughter in the past since Alinta was also still learning to read and write. She tucked the toddler in once she had nodded off and closed the door as she left. She knew the child would yell if she wanted out during the night. Fortunately, Ainia usually slept through the night now. Mel was grateful that no one knew what had happened to Alinta. What if Ainia had been with her? Would the man have hurt the child too?

Mel helped Alinta to the bathroom. Evidently, she hadn't used the bathroom very much in the week she had lain curled in their bed, and peeing hurt her. Mel asked to see between her legs and her wife reluctantly showed her. Mel saw the slight tears of the skin and tissue, which was why there had been blood on the sheets and why it hurt to pee. She had a thought, *If the man had raped her wife this way, had he done more?* She couldn't ask her wife and wouldn't probe further. Only another woman could understand how devastating this must be. Only another woman who had been raped could relate. Mel closed her eyes and prayed her wife wouldn't be permanently damaged by this attack. She loved her so, and she felt very guilty for being unable to be there for her and protect her.

That night, Mel just held Alinta safe in her arms, and for the first time since Mel had known her, she had nightmares. Mel's strong arms comforted and soothed her when she first woke and grasped at her.

Mel was surprised when Alinta insisted on getting up the next day and getting dressed, despite being weak. She was happy to see Ainia and acted as though nothing was wrong as she resumed her daily chores. Mel watched her and caught her looking about cautiously before going in dark places in the barns and sheds. She wished she could remove that fear, but she could only hover over her wife so much. Alinta's milk had dried up, and she slowly weaned Ainia off the woman who had so graciously fed her by increasing her intake of regular food. Alinta was obviously bothered by the fact that she couldn't provide this sustenance for her daughter anymore, and Mel could only watch and sympathize. She didn't have firsthand knowledge of the special bond between a mother and her baby.

The rain had moved off during the night, but the heat had returned, and a mist hung over the valley as rain that had been absorbed into the earth tried to burn off into the air. It was sultry and hot. Mel hated this kind of weather, but the danger of fire was eliminated wherever this storm had hit. Unfortunately, it didn't last long. More dry weather continued, and another fire sprang up on Twin Station a week later. Mel was reluctant to leave, but Alinta insisted. It was time they returned to their work. Mel had to take care of her station and help with their neighbor's station as they had helped her when the situation was reversed. Alinta knew it was time to put the horror of what had happened behind her and try to forget it. She was alive, and she had her daughter and her husband. She would forget everything. At least, that was what she told herself.

This time, Mel had two of the men stay behind, instructing them to keep their powder dry and guard the home station. Surprised, they took their orders as everyone else that was available got into the carts and headed out. Mel got on her horse and with one regretful look back at her wife standing on the porch with their daughter, she headed south to Twin Station.

CHAPTER TWELVE

Alinta was frightened watching Mel ride off. She was uncertain if her mate would come back, and she worried she might be attacked again while her husband was gone. She didn't sleep, and she barely ate, only forcing herself to eat because Ainia was watching her closely and wouldn't eat if her mother didn't. She was frightened of everything, staying in the house and starting whenever anyone came to the front door. Betty took to answering anytime a man knocked at the door. They were checking in regularly and were surprised that the missus wasn't answering the door. She was behaving oddly, and everyone was concerned. She barely did her share of the chores, letting others do them instead, but no one would question Alinta. It was maddening enough that Mel had ordered them to guard the home paddock. They would rather be off fighting the fire.

It began to rain in earnest, and this cheered everyone at the home paddock. They hoped that the rain had reached the far-off fire, and everyone would return home shortly.

Mel and the men and women who had gone to fight the fire were returning, and cheers went up among those who had been left behind. The rain had ended, and the sun came out from behind the clouds, casting a ray of sunshine on the house on the hill, the barns, and the sheds as well as the massive paddocks behind them. Alinta came out on the porch of their beautiful house and smiled gingerly, the skin around her mouth still hurting slightly as it healed. She waved enthusiastically to Mel, pleased to have her home.

"You needn't worry about that man anymore," Mel told her wife as she returned the hug they shared, despite Mel's grimy appearance. Alinta's eyes were black as she looked up at the larger woman. She waited for her to say more. "I killed him out in the paddock at Twin Station," she explained quietly, and Alinta gingerly touched the bruises she could see on Mel's face. "Well, we fought a little at first when he recognized me. I accused him of attacking you, then he fell into the fire as we fought, and he is gone now."

"For all time?" Alinta asked, looking hard at Mel. She had her own superstitions about fire and the hereafter.

"For all time," Mel reassured her, wishing she knew what her wife was thinking and feeling.

Alinta wasn't sure how she felt. She didn't spend time thinking about her feelings like the white woman. The man, she learned Bradley had been his name, was gone. Mel seemed unsure of herself in the coming weeks, and when months went by without them making love, Alinta didn't know how to heal the rift between them. She knew she

had been badly hurt, and as her young body healed, she wished she could forget. Having Mel home helped because she felt safe around the large woman.

She watched as the woman played with their daughter, sharing the kittens, who were teenagers now and long and lean. She was fascinated by these animals. They were sweet and made a purring sound, at least that is what Mel told her it was called. She had never heard an animal make these sounds before. It was strangely soothing, and she enjoyed holding them. Ainia sure liked these animals. Sometimes, she was sure she liked them more than the more rambunctious puppies.

She felt worse when Mel felt the need to ride off on some made up errand to Wilcannia, purportedly to take care of some business. She went alone, taking supplies to the stockmen in the folds along the track in that direction, not taking any of their stockmen and not offering to take Alinta. She was gone several weeks, and when she returned, she looked…determined. Alinta couldn't fathom what was changed about her husband. She didn't treat Alinta differently, she just seemed…different.

Strangely, it was Diablo she started seeing more when Mel had less time to attend to the young stallion with her duties out in the paddocks and around the station. At first, he had sniffed at the aboriginal woman with suspicion, but Mel told her to feed the animal carrots and hay, and when she did, she had found him behaving much more friendly toward her. He was still young in so many ways despite his adult size. He was rambunctious, playful, and hadn't yet achieved his full potential. He was causing problems with Mel's stallion, who sensed a rival for his mares and wanted to drive him out. They kept Diablo near the barns, and the herd of horses that Mel was cultivating were kept farther out in

the large valley hidden behind their house. The young stallion was lonely and welcomed the strange Aborigine with the delicious treats and cool, fresh water, who scratched his itchy coat as it grew thicker with the oncoming colder weather.

"Like this," Mel said, taking the time to teach Alinta how to groom the rambunctious horse. She was concerned at first that her wife would be trampled, but he eventually calmed down in Alinta's presence, and this surprised Mel. He was a magnificent addition to their herd, and her stallion wasn't happy. She discussed her concerns about the horses with her wife, trying not to talk about any of their problems as she sensed that Alinta didn't want to talk about the attack.

"Maybe he has his own wife?" Alinta asked as she carefully brushed the horse's lengthening hairs. She remembered when hair such as this would have been woven into more practical things. but she no longer needed bags and other things she would normally have made from this hair. Even the spinifex was cut down for the animals and no longer used to make things.

"That is a good idea. We can give him some mares of his own. You'll have to help me pick some from the herd," Mel offered, smiling at her wife for giving her the idea. "We should build a paddock of his own since we can't let him run in the valley with *him*," her chin indicated the valley where her herd stallion already held sway. "He'd challenge him and hurt him if he could," she explained.

"Maybe Diablo hurt him?" Alinta asserted, wanting to defend the younger horse, who was just trying to find his place.

"I don't think he's big enough yet, but it would be a shame to let him get hurt. If we just let him run with mares on his own, he would want more mares, and he would challenge the herd stallion for them."

Alinta nodded to show she understood what Mel was saying. Some of the men she had known in her tribe had two or three wives and would have taken more if they could have afforded it, although none had the riches of the white men she had seen. She glanced at Mel, wondering why this woman, who had the spirit of a man within her, had come into her life. She didn't understand it, but she accepted it and was grateful. She also didn't quite understand the love that Mel assured her she felt for her. She understood love between her and their daughter, but she found the love with Mel complicated. She felt bad that she hadn't been receptive to Mel's touches. Normally, she would have been making love with her, but since the attack that part of her was dead, and she didn't know if it would come back. She suspected her continued rejection of her husband was why she had made the trip to Wilcannia. She was content with the cuddles Mel gave her while holding her close and safe in her arms at night as they slept. At least it had stopped the nightmares…for now.

"Hey, boss," one of the men called, and Mel turned away since Alinta had the grooming well in hand. Diablo nibbled at her sleeve playfully as she rubbed his chest down with the brush. She smiled, pushing his muzzle away, so he wouldn't bite through the fabric. She had never thought of having an animal as a beast of burden when she was growing up, and the affection she felt for this animal surprised her. She was just finishing up and rubbing Diablo's last hoof with a rag as Mel had shown her when her husband returned.

"Want to go for a ride?" Mel asked.

"Ride?" she asked in return, looking beyond Mel to the mass of clouds on the horizon. It would rain soon as it had been doing with increasing frequency. If they went for a ride, she would have to bring

her sheepskins as they shed water well. Mel had made them for her from their own sheep that first rainy season. She dropped the hoof and patted the horse, picking up the things she had used and putting them away, so someone else could use them and she could find them the next time she wanted to groom.

"Yeah, Erickson was scouting about looking for more places where we could put a few folds to the north, and he discovered another valley. He says it's not as nice as ours," she gestured to the one behind the house. Their bedroom overlooked the beautiful valley, and she loved waking up to it daily. "I'd like to go up and check it out. Would you like to go with me? We could bring Ainia."

Alinta looked into Mel's brown eyes. She knew her husband was worried about her, but she just couldn't talk about the attack. It was in the past, and she wanted it to stay there. She hoped it would fade in time, and she didn't believe talking about it would solve any problems. She loved this big woman and knew she was trying to get them back to the closeness they once had. She knew they would once again make love, but she just hadn't been able to respond to the caresses yet; she wasn't ready. She would, however, please Mel in any other way she could. If going to see this valley pleased her husband, she would go with her. It would be good to take Ainia too. The little girl would love to be riding on a horse with her mother and father along. "Yes, we should go. I will go pack for us."

Mel smiled. She was pleased for an opportunity to get away with her little family. She turned to Erickson and said, "Pick out some fresh horses for us to ride, and I'll get the gear."

Alinta followed Mel, so she could take a couple saddle bags to fill with things they would need. She knew Mel would have stores from the stockroom in the packs, but she made sure to also pack some jerky and other emergency rations as Mel had taught her. She liked this concentrated and dried meat. It had many uses, and Mel had shown her how to make soups and even a stew using it. In turn, she had shown Mel some of the wild vegetables they could use, helping them live off the land much more effectively than using up their stores from the packs. It was healthy and nutritious, and she had loved that she could contribute just as much as the white woman. Alinta was getting excited about this little trip they would be taking, despite the expected rain.

The valley was much farther north than they had expected, and with their late start, they had to camp out two nights. They missed the rain, which went farther south, hitting the other end of the station, which badly needed the onslaught. Erickson was proud to show them this hidden valley, a bonus in an otherwise barren and desert-like region.

"I was following this game trail here," he indicated the path.

"Songtrail," Alinta murmured, but only Ainia heard her mother as she rode on the saddle before her. Mel was listening to her stockman as she memorized the way to the valley. They'd ridden all day to arrive here due to their late start the other day.

The path led between rocks and when the valley opened before them it was incredible. None of the sweltering heat from around them seemed to penetrate here. A stream ran down one side of the valley, and they could tell by the runoff that the water had forged this valley over the millennium. It went on for quite a way. There was a stand of trees filled with pigeons, cockatoos, and many other birds at one end, and luxurious grass ran the length of valley. Mel and Alinta allowed their horses to crop the long grasses, and Erickson told Mel what he had found.

"If we close off that end," he indicated beyond the stand of trees, "this would make a perfect paddock for sheep, and we don't have to put up a fold, although I think the sheep would feel safer if we did."

Mel nodded to show she was listening, but she was thinking this would be better for a herd of horses, and it would solve the problem of having two viable stallions in proximity. She could choose the mares that would go with Diablo, or maybe it would be better to move the older, unnamed stallion up here with his harem of mares.

"Let's look at the other end," she said agreeably, enjoying the stockman's enthusiasm as she looked about the large valley. "Any sign of dingoes?"

They didn't find any signs, and that was a good thing, but dingoes could be lurking anywhere. It was probably only a matter of time before the dingoes discovered this rich, luxurious valley, if they hadn't already. Native animals like emus and wallabies were evident, and the birds certainly made enough noise for everyone. The horses' ears flickered as they attempted to catch anything that might signal danger or an order from the humans riding them.

They explored the valley farther, finding that there was no other way into the valley where it narrowed into the high cliffs. One of the cliffs allowed the water to bubble out at its base, creating the stream that ran the length of the valley, digging slowly through the rocks and creating this beautiful valley.

"I guess the way in is also the way out," Mel stated as they explored, and Erickson agreed. "We won't need to close off that end," she indicated the cliffs. "Just put some bars across the rocks to keep the animals trapped in the valley."

"Who is going to want to be this remote though?" Erickson asked, expressing his own fears at the isolated valley. They both knew that some stockmen enjoyed being alone and others needed more people around. While acclimating to the Outback, some adapted better than others.

"Maybe that won't be an issue," Mel stated, thinking once again about horses instead of sheep, which wouldn't need to be watched as closely. Who did she have that could take on this chore for her? She wanted this valley as part of the station, and all she had to do was claim it.

They made camp. Erickson slept well away from the small family, so they could have their privacy. Ainia was uncharacteristically tired after their long ride and was running about in the grasses. Mel had played hide and seek in the grasses with her, chasing her and catching her in her arms, wearing her out with their play as Alinta watched and laughed at their antics. Their daughter looked so happy playing with the big woman. She wished she could join in, but she was feeling ill. The jerky hadn't settled right in her stomach.

That night, they lay on their bedrolls. Mel was behind Alinta, her arm around her wife protectively and Ainia on her own bed before her. She felt Mel's caresses, and when Mel would have stopped and pulled her arm back, Alinta grasped it and pulled it back. She sensed Mel's surprise. Alinta pulled the woman's hand down and ground against it slightly. The gasp she heard behind her made her smile, and she turned slightly as Mel looked at her, unsure if she should proceed after all these months. Instead, she captured the woman's lips, kissing her fervently and letting her know she wanted and needed her.

"Are you sure?" Mel asked as she started caressing her more intimately. She was glad they were far enough from the fire and in the shadows, so Erickson wouldn't see what they were doing.

"I want you, Mel," she admitted honestly.

"But–" Mel began, but Alinta silenced her with a kiss, her own hands reaching for Mel's trousers and unbuttoning them to reach inside. "Ohhhh," Mel gasped into Alinta's mouth, trying to stay quiet. Their child was only a few feet away. Alinta found what she was seeking, the folds of flesh moistening beneath her fingertips.

Mel couldn't believe her wife was initiating this after so long, but she soon realized she couldn't question a gift of this magnitude, and she quickly allowed her hands free rein on her wife's supple body, slipping up the long shirt and surprised at the summer underwear she was wearing beneath it. She quickly slipped inside it to find the warmth between Alinta's legs.

It had been too long for both women, and between the caresses, the kisses, and now the determined application of their fingers, they both came quickly under the Outback sky, smothering their moans of completion in each other's mouths.

Mel finally pulled away, wondering for a moment if they had ever come this quickly before and not caring. Alinta had reached for her, and she was thrilled.

Alinta had needed this closeness, not the thrusting of Mel's fingers but the touch that made her body feel those delicious tingles. Mel would never hurt her, and she had missed this. Alinta was thrilled that not only did Mel still want her after what she had been through, but her body was coming back to life after all this time. She kissed her again and again in gratitude, vaguely able to see her in what firelight reached into the dark here. She hugged her close, tugged her own clothes in order, and turned, pulling Mel's arm around her again as she cuddled close to her *husband's* bulk. She looked towards Ainia, checking on the little girl who lay there so contentedly. She wrapped her arm around the small girl, and it was at that exact moment that she felt movement for the first time. She knew Mel had felt it too as she stiffened and sat up to look down on her wife, peering at her through the darkness.

"Did you...?" she began and saw that Alinta had also felt the movement. At first, she looked shocked, then guilty, and finally, sad. "You're pregnant, aren't you?"

For the first time in her life, Alinta wanted to tell an untruth. She didn't know how though. She nodded, wondering if Mel would be angry with her. She had started to suspect something about a week ago but hadn't really thought much about it. Instead, to her amazement Mel's brown eyes, visible in the light of the fire, looked at her with an unfathomable look.

"Are you happy to be having a baby?" Mel cautiously asked. Her heart was pounding.

Alinta didn't want to shake her head, and remembering how the white people shrugged, she didn't want to do that either. "I don't know," she answered honestly.

"Because of how it was conceived?"

Alinta hadn't really thought about that. Of course, she knew now how Ainia had been conceived. She wasn't naive anymore. She hadn't thought about the fact that when Bradley had beaten and raped her again it could possibly result in a child. Her eyes grew huge as she thought of what Mel had just asked. Then, she realized in that instant that Mel would never be able to give her a child of her own body. This would be their last chance for another child. "I hadn't…" Alinta began haltingly.

"If you don't want it, I know there are things you could take, but this would be ours…" Mel tried not to sound desperate or pleading, but she worried as Alinta had been depressed and too quiet for a while now. She wanted the baby, and at the same time she wanted Alinta to be healthy and happy. She felt she had failed this amazing woman and wanted somehow to make it up to her.

Alinta had never thought of that. She knew there were plants she could take to end the pregnancy, but she wasn't certain which ones they were. Her knowledge of the native plants didn't extend that far. She could probably figure it out since some plants were purgatives, and with enough of them…No! She wouldn't do that. This was her child. Bradley had nothing to do with Ainia beyond her conception. This child would also be her child, and he would never bother her again, Mel had seen to that. Mel, her husband-wife, would protect her and protect them in any way she could. She would be a wonderful father to this unknown child.

In a flash, she saw Mel playing with Ainia in the field, catching her up and giggling with the little girl, and she knew that this child would be loved and wanted. Alinta made a negative sign with her hand in response to the question about the plants, and Mel saw it in the firelight. "This is our child," she said simply and saw the smile Mel gave her. She had thought their smiles a grimace the first few times she saw it on the white people's faces until she realized it conveyed joy. She returned Mel's smile, realizing that they would have another baby, probably about the same time of year Ainia had been born several years ago, right after the sheep dropped their lambs. Her hand went to her stomach where she and Mel had felt the movement, and she shared a look with the American woman. They would be having a baby together.

CHAPTER THIRTEEN

Mel was especially solicitous of Alinta as they headed back early the next morning. "Are you sure you should be riding?" she asked, completely forgetting the fact that her wife had ridden all during her pregnancy with Ainia. "Should I have Ainia on my horse?"

Ainia, hearing that, naturally wanted to ride with Mel, and Alinta handed her off willingly. The little girl was sick of riding and had been wiggly. Perhaps Mel could keep her in check. Ainia listened as Mel and Erickson discussed the valley.

"We need to find a stockman who can handle horses. I want to use that valley for that new stallion of ours."

"Maybe your older stallion? He could keep away the predators, who are sure to find the valley with more goings and comings through

that," he pointed to where they had just come through the hidden entranceway.

Mel nodded, acknowledging that someone might have more knowledge of this than her. "We'll have to put a fence along that end to keep them from getting out," she mentioned.

"Well, if you put horses here, that stallion can keep them, and there ain't enough grass up here," he indicated the rolling plains they were now on, "to keep a very large flock. Any stockman could check on the herd."

Mel agreed thoughtfully, envisioning it, and then, they found exactly where the permanent fold should go. Unsure if the billabong was permanent or fed from the springs in the valley, they staked out where it should go and discussed it further. Alinta helped as they pounded in the stakes, watching amused as Mel held her horse by its reins with the toddler holding on to the pommel proudly, sure she was riding the horse all by herself. The little girl looked so noble up on the saddle, the little dress shirt they had made for her spread out over both her legs on the saddle as she held on.

"Okay, there's that chore done," Mel said as they pounded in the last stake. "We'll send a crew up here to make the fold and ask who would like the job," she said to Erickson as she helped Alinta up on her horse, her hand lingering in affection on her wife's thigh as she looked up at her meaningfully, sharing a little smile of affection.

Alinta shared that smile, feeling so good inside herself about her mate's love. She watched Mel mount her own horse, effortlessly controlling the animal as she got in the saddle behind their daughter. Her arms went around the toddler, firmly grasping the reins.

"Know any of the men who would like this position?" Mel asked Erickson, who shook his head thoughtfully.

They discussed the new fold and the valley. Mel was pleased with the find and was giving Erickson full credit for it. As they discussed which of the horses they would choose to bring up here, Alinta voiced her opinion that the older, more experienced stallion would be a better choice to defend his mares against predators.

By the time they rode back to the station, things were pretty much decided. The return trip didn't take nearly as long, and when they were dismounting, Mel said to Erickson, "Gather a crew to go up there and build that fold tomorrow. I'll have parts of a couple flocks brought up there. I think you are right, and we shouldn't have a large flock with that growth."

"I'll gather the tools and have everything ready for first thing in the morning," he agreed as they handed their mounts off to of the young grooms, who ran up to take them.

Alinta took Ainia from Mel. The child had fallen asleep in the woman's arms. "Better wake her, so she can eat dinner and go to bed," Mel suggested with a grin.

"She mighty tuckered from the ride and your snacks," she teased her husband as she looked fondly down at their daughter. Mel had been sneaking things from her saddlebags to feed the toddler as they rode, the adults eating jerky to tide them over, so they could be home well before dark.

"Whose horses are those?" Mel asked, looking in one of the corrals.

Pete Winston came walking up. "Find something we can use?" he asked.

"Aye, Erickson found us a right useful valley for the extra horses and one of the stallions. We staked out a fold near a billabong nearby. Erickson is loading up tools now, and I want you two to choose some of the men to go build it. It'd probably be best if Erickson went up again as he knows where it is." She saw the head stockman stiffening as she assigned some of his duties to another man. "I want you to trim one or two of the flocks that might be too big for some of the folds and send those sheep up there. By the time you get a good-sized flock together, they should have the fold well along. Have the men going with Erickson take all but a couple of the mares and the herd stallion and put them in the valley he found." The man settled down, realizing that the boss was trusting him with choosing the sheep for this new fold as well as giving him orders once again. Erickson wasn't taking his job. "Whose horses are those?" Mel asked, nodding towards the fine mounts she saw in one of the corrals.

"Oh, you have some visitors. They are up in the house," he said offhand as he waited to be dismissed, so he could help Erickson prepare for the trip.

Mel nodded to acknowledge him, now curious about who was visiting their remote station. They didn't get visitors too often, and she glanced once again at the horses in the corral, wondering if they were from Twin Station, the only place visitors had come from in the past. "I'll talk to you tomorrow before you leave."

He nodded, hurrying off.

Mel took Alinta's outstretched hand. She had waited for her husband, and Mel smiled down at the sleepy child in her wife's arms. Alinta looked around the busy station. The grooms were taking the saddles off the horses they had ridden, someone was throwing feed to

the chickens in the pen, and she could hear the ducks and geese down by the creek setting up an evening cacophony of noise along with the cockatoos and other birds in the trees. A horse whinnied from the corrals and a cow answered. She could even hear the pigs grunting happily as someone fed them. She was happy. This was home, and for perhaps the first time in her life, she understood the concept of a home. She looked up at the house Mel had built for them. This was their house, and she was pleased to be here. She could forget what had happened to her in the house because her future was with Mel, and she looked down again at their daughter, conscious of the life inside her that they would also share. She was very, very happy!

Mel felt the same way. It was almost as though she could read Alinta's mind as she also looked about their place. The lawns they now had were not yet scorched by the hot summer's sun, and they were kept trimmed by the youths she hired to care for them. She'd shocked a few people by allowing girls and boys to do the same work. She saw no reason they couldn't do the job if they knew how to do the work. She wouldn't allow some of they younger children to touch a scythe, but they could feed the chickens, ducks, geese, and pigs. The place looked well kept, and there were no weeds around the posts of the various corrals and pens. Even the rails on these corrals and pens had been painted and looked bright against the evening sky. God, she loved the Outback. It was beautiful, and she understood better understood what Alinta had told her before…she didn't own this land, the land owned her. She walked with her wife and child up the steps, a cat arching as it stretched and yawned from where it had been sleeping. She grinned at the lazy creature. They had only lost one of the kittens, and those that remained were doing the job she had hoped they would.

"Guess we can just put her to bed," Mel said as she looked at their daughter and opened the door to let Alinta enter before her.

"No wash?" Alinta asked, surprised since Mel was normally adamant about such things, and Alinta had thought of them as white things, something she wanted for their daughter.

"Well, maybe–" she began but stopped talking as she saw their guest in the doorway of the sitting room.

"Hello, Melissa," the woman said, and Mel stopped dead in her tracks, staring at the incongruous view of Lady Abigail Baxter standing in her house. She mentally corrected herself, it was Lady Worthington now.

"Abigail?" she asked, not sure she wasn't seeing things.

Alinta looked at the immaculately dressed woman standing in their home, and she immediately sensed this was not a good thing for her or for *them*.

"I go by the name Mel now," she hastily corrected the woman, hoping that no one had overheard Abigail and she hadn't given away Mel's secret. It was vitally important for people to think of her as Mel Lawrence out here, not Melissa. Looking away, she saw that Abigail had looked directly at her wife. "This is my wife, Alinta and our daughter, Ainia," she introduced her.

Abigail stiffly nodded towards the aboriginal woman and didn't even glance at the toddler held in her arms.

"I take Ainia up," Alinta said quickly, sensing she didn't really want to be here for this.

Both Mel and Abigail watched the woman, who was dressed in an oversized man's shirt and leather boots, mount the stairs carrying the toddler. Mel turned to look at Abigail, noting she was dressed as

befitted a noblewoman of her station. It looked totally out of place here in the Outback where they were much more casual. She looked older, more mature, even taller, and Mel could feel the old attraction, but she was conflicted as her wife climbed the stairs with their child. "What are you doing here?" she asked, putting her hat on the stand next to the door and noting the hat on another hook and assuming it was Abigail's.

"That's all you can say after all these years? No hug of welcome? Nothing more?" Abigail asked, her upper crust British tones sounding odd to Mel's ears after years of hearing the Australian twang and Alinta's pidgin English.

Mel smiled at Abigail, pleased to see her looking so well but not really thrilled to have her here in the home where she lived with her wife. "It's been a lot of years, Abigail, or should I call you Lady Worthington?"

"You may call me Abigail, you know that," she said, feeling disappointed that Mel wasn't more welcoming. "My husband is dead. I'm now the Dowager Lady Worthington."

"I'm sorry to hear that. Your letter said you were interested in Australia, but I certainly never expected to see you here."

"You know why I'm here," she stated, looking at Mel meaningfully.

"No," she shook her head, "I don't. What are you doing here, Abigail?"

"I'm here for you, Melis–" she stopped herself, amending it to Mel before she could finish. "I came here to be with you."

Alinta, listening at the top of the stairs, felt a clutch in her heart at those words.

THE END

About the Author

K'Anne Meinel is the BEST-SELLING author of LAWYERED, REPRESENTED, SAPPHIC SURFER, DOCTORED, VEIL OF SILENCE, SURVIVORS, VETTED and CAVALCADE as well as several other books including her first, SHIPS which was written in 2003 over the course of two weeks. A gypsy at heart, she has lived in many locations and plans to continue roaming. Videos of several of her books are available on YouTube outlining some of the locations of her books and telling a little bit more…giving the readers insight into her mind as she created these wonderful stories. As of this date she has more than 100 published works including shorts, novellas, and novels. She is an American author born in Milwaukee, Wisconsin and raised in Oconomowoc. Upon early graduation from high school she went to a private college in Milwaukee and then moved to California for seventeen years before returning to the state. Many of her stories have Wisconsin in them as settings for her wonderful, realistic, and detailed backgrounds. Named the lesbian Danielle Steel of her time, K'Anne continues to write interesting stories in a variety of genres in both the lesbian and mainstream fiction categories. Her website is www.kannemeinel.com.

If you have enjoyed **OUTBACK NATIVE**, I hope you will enjoy this
excerpt from
OUT AT THE INN

Among the majestic shoreline of the Central Coast of California lies a secret...Leah Van Heusen finds a hidden staircase....

The ancient house she finds among the overgrown foliage is amazing...and eerie, most wouldn't even step a foot closer but she is intrigued and feels drawn to the old mansion....

Leah finds more than she bargains for after seeking out the owner and purchasing the entire estate for a dollar. As she starts to restore it, she finds out who her real friends are, she also finds out who her family really is...What's a few ghosts between friends?

Between repairs, upgrades, and finding out the houses secrets, Leah has her hands full. Finding out her sexuality and dating is the least of her worries. As her beloved dream of an Inn becomes reality she finds it suddenly in jeopardy, who will kill for it or the immense fortune that she has found?

CHAPTER ONE

Leah probably would never have seen the staircase if it wasn't for D.O.G. and Speck playing around on the beach among the rocks that had fallen from the cliffs over the years. She had hiked this stretch of beach dozens of times in the past but had never noticed the nearly hidden staircase leading up the cliffs. Looking at what they were avidly sniffing at, she wondered if they had found some more sea grass or crabs or something dead, like a fish. She wrinkled her nose in distaste at the thought as they snuffled around at the cliff base, and she looked up in astonishment. As she examined it, she realized how expertly it fit into the various nooks and crannies of the cliff, effectively camouflaging it against the stone. She wondered where it led. It had to be pretty old by the weathering she saw on the wood that remained, but then anything left exposed to the elements on a beach weathered quickly. She realized the last ten feet or so had been washed away, probably from high tide, surf, or the many storms that hit this section of the coast. In fact, none of the staircase should be here, she thought, as she examined it. Yet, she realized the builder had taken advantage of the natural overhang of the cliff to protect and hide it, using the stone whenever possible. Unless you knew it was there, it wouldn't be found. She found it clever and intriguing.

It was the intriguing part that had her hesitating. No one knew she was here except for the dogs. She wanted to climb up and find where the staircase led to. That meant the possibility of danger. It also meant hauling the dogs up the side of a cliff on a staircase that who knew how old or creaky, stable, or dangerous it was. She sighed. She hated having to think it out: she was more of a spur of the moment kind of gal and she wanted to explore where this led. It was a path she hadn't known was there, and she wanted to see where it ended. The child in her, the adventurer, was very captivated.

She sighed again. Just then D.O.G, pronounced deeooogee, showed up to see where she was. He spotted her staring up at the climb between the bottom of the stairs and the beach where they had been walking. Speck saw D.O.G. locating their human and trotted over to see what was interesting them both so much, not wanting to be left out. They watched their human to see what new adventure they would be participating in soon, and they knew they *would be* participating—Leah never left them out. Whether it was a walk on the beach, or a ride in her Jeep with the top down, they were always up for that, and they were partners in crime. They obeyed her, of course, but she wasn't too bossy a human to cohabitate with, and they loved her dearly. Both dogs could see the stairway but didn't think too much of it. It was a human thing. Why it was ten feet off the ground didn't make sense to their canine brains, but then humans could be confusing.

Leah knew she couldn't resist. Even though she didn't have climbing tools, even though she didn't have any gear other than her sweat shirt jacket, jeans, and sports shoes, she was going to make that climb *and* find where these steps led. Something was compelling her to do it. Something was telling her that this was a path she had to follow. Gear and safety be damned! It wouldn't be the first time, and she was certain it wouldn't be the last time either. It was her day off, and she had been enjoying it with her two fur kids. This path had come into her otherwise complacent life for a reason, and who was she to ignore it? Besides, she wasn't sure she could find it again. She examined the crumbling rock from the cliff face and realized a path she could climb to the steps with relatively minor discomfort. She also realized that the two dogs would probably follow her and be able to climb the same path just as well, which would alleviate the lifting of two full grown and heavy beasts.

Taking a deep breath, a delighted one at the challenge, she began to walk towards the crumbling stones and decide where to put her feet as she began to ascend towards the staircase. Slowly, she moved forward and upward as she made her way. Both dogs delighted in this new and different adventure that their human had decided on. They didn't care where they were going; they were going to go together and that was what mattered. D.O.G. in his usual exuberant and indomitable way attempted to get ahead of the group and climb but found his way blocked by stones too high to climb easily—he had to turn back. Speck laughed at him in his own canine way with his tongue hanging out and his tail wagging. In canine language, he was saying, *"See, you should have waited for our human to show the way, you fool!"* and laughed joyously to see his partner in crime getting stuck and having to return.

Leah slowly made her way up. It had really crumbled here and the footfalls were many—so were the chances of slipping off a rock and breaking her ankle or worse. She managed to get to the bottom stair but found it would be better to climb a little more and take the next one. The last one must have been from a set and was ready to fall to the beach at any moment. Once on the stairway, though, she found it to be sturdily built and the handrail was part of the cliff as well as interspersed with thick sturdy wood. Who would have built this and why? She began to climb the stairs with the two dogs that had made the climb with her, trotting up and passing her to see what they could find before her and in competition with each other. They were soon up the next flight and the next before her.

She called, "No fair, you have four paws and I only have two!" Both dogs glanced back to see if she was calling them back, but as she continued to carefully climb the steps towards them and check her footing, she ignored them. They turned as one and continued their ascent.

Leah looked back and could clearly see the stairwell leading down to the beach. She could also see why it had been hidden from the beach the way it wound into the cliff face as a part of the rock and not on the outside of it. Whoever the builder was had been a genius in their use of mother nature. In fact, periodically she could swear there was some sort of planter's boxes, or what she assumed were planter's boxes. There was nothing in them but debris, and most were rotted clean away. She really admired it until her foot went through one of the steps and brought her mind back to the present and the fact that she was climbing this ancient thing and should really pay attention. Who knew how old this thing was or whether it really did go the whole way up. She might find another ten-foot section missing when she got to the top of this thing. She wasn't looking forward to that idea but the staircase continued, and she was pleasantly surprised when it came out by some low boulders on the top of the cliff that were weather worn but sturdy.

She looked around. The dogs were sniffing out some bushes and trees, making their marks. She was surprised at how profuse the foliage was. Normally this section of the coast was beaten down by the storms and the winds. Then she realized it had all been planted—not a lot of native vegetation was growing here. It was all very overgrown, of that she could see. It was sadly neglected, too. She called the dogs to her, thinking that there were probably rattlesnakes or tarantulas in that mess, and she didn't want to walk alone through it as they explored. She and the dogs would be in it together this way. And they would explore it. She was too intrigued to find out what this planted mess was hiding.

She realized that there had been some type of lawn under these trees at one time and that the bushes, some of them in flower, were not native to the Central Coast. They all needed massive trimming, and she became more intrigued when she found no set path to follow as they explored.

She was getting irritated by the high grasses and low branches. Imagining spiders and snakes around every bush and tree, she had decided to head back when she spied among the foliage the outline of a house. She wracked her brain to remember what house was situated along this section of the coast and couldn't for the life of her remember any such house. This was a long stretch of nothing that had stood here for thousands of years with nobody but cows, sheep, or whatever grazing on it. To find this little oasis of overgrown abundance had been a surprise, but the house that stood hidden among this jungle was astonishing...and interesting.

Leah looked at it. It was dark and dreary and nearly hidden with vines, trees, and branches covering it as mother nature attempted to take it back to the Earth. Someone had built a fine house of native stones and then left it. That alone fascinated her romantic heart. Something was niggling at the back of her mind as she took it all in, but she suppressed it as she gazed in wonder at the three-story edifice before her. It was pretty large, but the warm climate and the unchecked growth of the trees, bushes, and grasses had taken over. She could see where a couple of branches had broken in windows on the second and possibly the third floors. Slowly, she made her way up small hills and around the house. She could see only slightly inside. The windows were filthy with time, dust, and debris. It only captivated her further. The dogs were enjoying themselves immensely, snuffling in the leaves and grasses that had accumulated for who knew how long. Leah still looked around, wondering if they would see any wildlife and hoped that no spiders or snakes were about. When the dogs scared up a couple of birds, it frightened the hell out of her, and she jumped. The house and it's eerily quiet foreboding presence was giving her the heebie-jeebies.

When she got around to the front of the large house, which seemed to take forever, she was pleasantly surprised to find it looked like something out of the Walton's from television with its wide welcoming porch that spanned the entire front. The wood was aged, and its patina beautiful. The native stone against the house complimented the two different materials, giving the front porch a cool, come and sit look. The huge windows had a wonderful view of what must have been a delightful and unique view of the Santa Lucia Mountains. Now it was just as overgrown as the backyard, and she couldn't see the upper stories at all from the growth. Leah could see where a circular driveway had once stood, and she wondered when this place had been built and why it was abandoned. Off to one side, she could see what was a large carriage house or barn; she couldn't be sure which with all the rich growth hiding it from view. She turned back to the house and wondered if she should go in. Something inside of her was encouraging her to do so. Logically, she knew she was trespassing, but the something was pushing her to look more, to see more, to explore. Plus, she hadn't seen any signs warning her away from the property—perhaps they were out front, wherever that was along this stretch of the coast. She glanced up at the sky, having to look practically straight up to see the position of the sun. She knew she had plenty of daylight left, but she didn't have a flashlight and didn't want to stay too late. The thought of using those steps in the dark did not appeal at all.

Still, she was compelled to go on. Wicker furniture stood all over the front porch, as though waiting for someone to come and sit. Something had nested in several of the chairs as the padding had been pulled out and used. The dogs came to investigate and preceded her up the stone stairs to the wide porch. Both of them thoroughly snuffled the nests they came across. Leah put her head up to the window and, cupping her hand above her face, tried to see in. Faintly, she could see into the dark rooms, but there was too much grime on the windows and many of them on this level had shutters firmly closed. She tried and failed on each of the wide overly large windows. She hesitated and then tried the great front double set of doors, but they were firmly locked. From the dust and blown leaves and things, it had been a very long time since anyone had been here. It only stirred her imagination even more as she tried and failed repeatedly to look inside.

It was on the far side of the house in what must be a pantry that she found a window that had been broken by a falling branch. The branch was pretty decent sized and still lodged halfway into the window with its other end resting on the ground. Leah tugged on it, but it was very heavy and barely moved. She climbed it carefully, much to the amusement of her canines. Then they became alarmed when they realized she might be going someplace without them. Slowly, she crawled up the leaning branch and could see slightly in the window, but the branch was too large and filled the window—she couldn't get by. There wasn't enough room to squeeze in, but she could see in. It was a small room which fortunately had a door that was firmly shut. Apparently, this room had been used by a generation of rodents of some kind or perhaps raccoons because a lot of debris had been hauled or blown in. It was a mess from what little she could see. D.O.G. attempted to balance on the leaning branch to join her, and she ordered him down. He looked crushed but obeyed. She hopped down from her perch and realized she could have broken something very easily while she was pretty far from civilization.

She looked around the entire house but found no loose window, open shutter, or unlocked door. She cursed whoever was keeping her from the place and then laughed. Wasn't the whole point of a locked house to keep intruders out? It was a terrific looking house, and she was intrigued. She wondered idly if it was for sale and then laughed at herself again. It was obviously abandoned, but by whom?

She made her way over to what proved to be an enormous carriage house. This was unlocked, and she was able to swing wide the doors. She could see actual carriages, a bit dusty but still in their element, inside. She was surprised to see a tarped car as well, and pulling off part of it, she recognized an old Model A or something of that sort. She had no idea but appreciated the look of the antique. It was a burgundy colored model, and the tarp had kept it very clean. She replaced it carefully. Looking around, she could see the same well-built appearance of the house put into this carriage house. More wood had been used on it but the native stone was present in each of the corners, as though a chimney had been built to hold it all together. It was beautiful, and she appreciated it. It was also dusty and getting late, so she reluctantly called off the interested and nosy dogs and closed it back up firmly, leaving it as she had found it.

Walking down what must have been a beautifully tended driveway at some point, she came out of the jungle abruptly to see where a stream had cut across the drive and gradually over time had cut into the dirt and rock, cutting off the drive from the rest of the long track that she could faintly see led towards the mountains. It was completely dry now. In between the drive and the mountains, of course, was Pacific Coast Highway which she could see must be beyond another mini jungle at the end of this drive. People must have noticed it from P.C.H. over the years but probably assumed this large field was held for cattle or something as those on the hills were. She looked around curiously, wondering if she herself could spot it from the highway and probably had driven by here on her way to various hiking spots up in Big Sur over the years and never noticed it.

The dogs looked like they wanted to cross the creek, so she turned back to the jungle and made her way back to the house, pushing aside branches along the track as well as ducking when necessary. She looked at the house a long time, watching as the dogs pounced in their eternal hunt for whatever. She suspected a mouse at this moment but didn't worry about those in her excitement over discovering this abandoned house. Slowly, she made her way back to the steps down the cliff. It seemed a very long time, rather days and weeks, since she had discovered them with the dogs, more than the mere hours she had been up here. She felt like she had discovered more than an abandoned house; she felt like she had found something, but it still niggled at the back of her mind and wouldn't become a coherent thought.

Carefully, she made her way down the steep steps envying the dogs and their four legs at this moment. It was abrupt but well-made, and she could see the workmanship that had gone into the making of this hidden staircase as well as the stairwell itself. Some of it was carved out of the actual cliff stone. It showed incredible craftsmanship. It made her wonder why no one else had seen it, but then she remembered how well hidden it actually was. Even she who knew where it was had a hard time seeing it again once she was on the beach. She carefully looked around, memorizing where it was and trying to remember the rock formations where they had found it. She had a feeling it was like that movie called *Brigadoon* with Gene Kelly or something, and it would all be gone tomorrow when the mists cleared. It only appeared once every hundred years or so.

As Leah made her way back down the beach, she felt kind of buoyant, almost as though she was floating on air, and she wasn't sure exactly why. She thought about the abandoned house over and over again. Since tomorrow was Sunday, she decided she would get an early start and try to find it from the highway. She made her way back to the Jeep, remembering at the last moment to put both dogs on their leads and pretend they had been on them their entire walk. As they walked up to where she had parked her Jeep on this windswept and remote part of the beach, she saw no one around. It never paid to push the rules too much, so she kept the dogs on their leads. Both of them heeled perfectly.

Stopping at the Jeep, both dogs sat expectantly. Leah brushed them down, getting most of the sand off of them, before allowing them to jump into the back of the Jeep despite the wet paws and the sand they still brought with them. She shrugged. Part of having dogs was having messes, and a Jeep was perfect for two healthy dogs that enjoyed the hiking and other things that she did. The SUV was just a part of their lifestyle, and she didn't sweat it if the backseat was dirty, dog dirty, because these were her fur kids.

She drove slowly south. Traffic on this Saturday was light on this stretch of P.C.H., and she made her way past San Simeon and towards Cambria. Missy would have dinner on for them both if she hadn't decided they should go out, and she looked forward to it. Her excursions today had made her hungry. She thought about what she had done, what she had seen, what she'd like to see more of, and round and round it went in her head as she made her way south, and the sun set to her right. She pulled into Cambria and behind some trees just as the sun set, and it was instantly dark. The hills between Cambria with their tall pine trees and the ocean made it feel like a mountain retreat. She pulled down Ocean Boulevard and made her way to Missy's home.

Both dogs jumped out when she parked and opened the door for them, familiar with this home away from home.

"D.O.G.!" one of the twins called.

"Speck!" the other one called when they saw the two dogs.

Leah grinned. She loved that the girls loved her dogs as much as she did because the dogs loved them both right back. She watched as they hugged the appropriate dog and then switched to make sure no one was jealous or left out. For six-year-olds, they could really hug hard and both dogs loved every moment of it as their happy expressions and wagging tails would attest.

"Hey sailor, where ya been?" Missy asked as she came into the living room from the kitchen.

Leah laughed as she looked up from where the twins were greeting their fur cousins. "Hey, what's cooking, Mother Hubbard? Smells great!"

"Ach, you say that all the time. You just want to stay on my good side so I feed you!" Missy teased.

Leah nodded as she followed her friend back into the kitchen where a toddler of three was walking around, and seeing Leah, slipped by her to look for the dogs. "Nice to see you, too, Breton," she said with a smile, knowing the dogs were the attraction. She looked at the other kid in the room, tied in his high chair and banging a spoon as he fed himself applesauce or something equally goopy, because he was covered in it from his nose to his chest. "Hey, Bradley, looks like you've been eating dinner," she said unnecessarily and was rewarded with a three-toothed grin of greeting.

"Yeah, I decided if I fed him and Breton early, the rest of us might get some peace during our dinner," Missy answered as she deftly cleaned up the squirming tot with a washcloth.

Bradley didn't want his face wiped and turned from his mother's towel filled hand as he looked over at Leah and tried to see beyond her.

Leah wasn't fooled. She knew Bradley wouldn't be happy to see her alone; it was the dogs that drew him, and he wouldn't be content until he had pulled and prodded both of the dogs who would enjoy every minute of it as they helped the little boy learn how to walk. How they knew that he was getting his balance, Leah didn't know, but they were self-appointed helpers and seemed not to mind when he pulled a little too hard on their hair or fell on them. Leah had even picked up Bradley a few times when he burrowed in and fell asleep on them. They didn't object. They loved the kids. She often wondered if she was depriving her fur kids by not having any human ones of her own, but seeing how exhausted they often were on the way home, she suspected they didn't miss having children of their own *that* much.

"Anything I can do to help?" Leah offered and found herself washing dishes *before* dinner because Missy hadn't had time to finish them from breakfast, and Leah suspected some from the night before as well.

While D.O.G. and Speck entertained Bradley from the safety of the playpen and allowed him to pull their hair and try to pat them, only getting out of reach occasionally when his exuberance to pull them into the pen hurt them with his fistfuls of hair. His calls and cookie brought them back and Leah winced as they shared. It never fazed Missy that her son was eating the cookie and allowing the dogs to have it too, soon though, the dogs had eaten it all.

The five of them were sitting at Missy's kitchen table with Breton still eating a little now and then before toddling back into the living room to take Bradley another cookie and pat the dogs.

"I swear those dogs are better baby sitters than that gal Carrie I pay to watch the kids now and then," Missy commented as she watched the children.

Leah shook her head. She only had two fur kids and Missy had four human ones. How she managed was a wonder. A nearly single mother, her husband Jack was on the road four out of seven days a week for a development firm out of Los Angeles who had opened an office in San Luis Obispo. Why they lived up here in Cambria, another forty miles away, Leah didn't understand, but Jack wanted the cool air and the distance from the 'big city' for his kids to grow up in. The fact that he only enjoyed it occasionally didn't faze him. Missy was raising the four nearly single handedly, and Leah admired her for it.

"So, where'd you go today? I thought you said you'd be back before sundown," Missy asked halfway through their delicious meal of roast that Leah had brought with her from the store last night when she arrived from Los Angeles. It was large enough that there would be plenty of leftovers for Missy and the kids the next couple of days as she made various meals from it.

"I went to a beach above San Simeon and hiked north along the beach from there."

"Aren't those elephant seals up there?" Missy frowned in worry, looking like a mother hen with her feathers ruffled.

Leah laughed at the mental image she had of her friend but didn't do it aloud. Missy wouldn't have appreciated the comparison, and she felt every one of her three pregnancies and complained that she hadn't lost any of the pounds she had put on from them.

"No, it's the wrong time of the year for them that's why I went up there."

"Did you go as far as Jade Beach or did you go further into Big Sur?"

Leah shook her head. "No, I stopped before that, shortly after Hearst Castle."

"Bet it was pretty up there," Misty said wistfully. For her, packing up four kids was too much work, so she tried not to do it too often. Between bottles and baby gear and miscellaneous, it was an expedition to go anywhere for her.

"It was; I found something interesting, too."

"Oh really?" Missy said in a teasing voice. "A man washed up on shore?"

Leah laughed. It had been an ongoing joke for them for years ever since Jack had washed up in front of them and fallen not for the leggy brunette that was Leah but for the short and stout Missy with the freckles and the dimples. He had been surfing and broke his board on the rocks off the Central Coast and pulled himself onto the beach to land at Missy's feet, almost literally. "No, I found a secret staircase," she teased back, knowing her friend wouldn't believe her.

"Uh huh, and did it lead up to heaven?" she asked as she gave Bradley two cookies this time, and he turned back to take them to his brother and ended up feeding both dogs.

"Why don't you just put them in their food dish and call it square?" Leah asked as she watched her friend indirectly feed her dogs the treats.

"Then it wouldn't wear out Bradley," she replied matter of factly.

To Leah, that made sense. Wearing out the boys was a full-time job. With the twins taking up so much of Missy's time and effort, too, all the kids seemed to pull her in so many directions. It was exhausting to watch.

"So, what did you really find that kept you so late? Maybe you should give me the coordinates in the future, so if I have to send out a search party, we have something to go on."

"I really did find a hidden staircase." Leah went on to tell her of her adventures, talking over and around four little kids who interrupted, demanded attention, and needed help cutting their food.

Missy listened enthralled. She was envious, and yet she had the kids to keep her busy. It would have exhausted her and her rotund body to hike down that beach much less climb up the staircase. The thought of finding an abandoned house was exciting but also alarming. What could have happened to her friend if she had gotten in the house and fallen through the floor or something? And what if it really wasn't abandoned and instead some hermit lived there and had shot her or something worse? Her mind thought a million times a minute as she was in 'mom' mode. "Are you crazy? What if something had happened to you?"

"Then D.O.G. and Speck could have pulled a Lassie routine and returned here to get you and take you to the well where I fell down and had to spend the night, shivering with the cold, ending up with pneumonia where you would have to feed me broth from this delicious roast, watched over by my faithful companions." She glanced at the dogs that were attentively watching the cookie brigade.

"You're nuts. You could have had something awful happen to you."

"I'm going back," Leah answered before shoving a cut potato into her mouth.

"Alone?" Missy said alarmed.

Leah nodded. "I'll take the boys." She nodded to the dogs in the next room, and for a moment, Missy wasn't sure she meant her fur kids but rather Breton and Bradley.

"Why?" Missy asked as she was relieved to realize the absurdity of her friend taking two little boys and realizing she meant the dogs.

Leah shrugged. "I want to get there when there is more light, and I'm going to try to get in there from the road. Have you ever heard of this house?" She described what she had seen again, giving Missy the willies at the sound of this 'abandoned' house.

"No, and I don't think you should go back. It's in the middle of nowhere. What if something happened?"

"I'm not going to do anything that will endanger myself. I'm just going to look. I think I might be able to drive in with the track. It's a little overgrown, but I'm sure the Jeep can handle it."

"You're nuts. You take unnecessary chances," Missy said as she handed the twins napkins to wipe their faces.

"Hey, what happened to the chick who used to be my backup on these adventures?"

"She grew up and grew responsible," Missy retorted a little more forcefully than she meant to.

"I did, too. Just not in the way you did," Leah answered quietly.

Missy looked over at her best friend and felt instantly sorry for her quick words. "I'm sorry. That wasn't what I meant and you know it."

Leah smiled ruefully. "Don't sweat it."

They discussed other things, most centering around the children that had interrupted them throughout the meal, and dropped the subject of the abandoned house for now.

TO BE CONTINUED...

~End sample chapter of OUT AT THE INN~
For more go to www.Shadoepublishing.com to purchase
the complete book or for many other delightful offerings

~ Because a publisher should stand behind their authors~

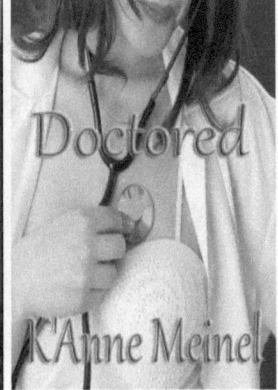

www.shadoepublishing.com

What do you do when you meet someone who changes everything you know about love and passion?

Paige Harlow is a good girl. She's always known where she was going in life: top grades, an ivy league school, a medical degree, regular church attendance, and a happy marriage to a man. Falling in love with her gorgeous roommate and best friend Alyssa Torres is no small crisis. Alyssa is chasing demons of her own, a medical condition that makes her an outcast and a family dysfunctional to the point of disintegration make her a questionable choice for any stable relationship. But Paige's heart is no longer her own. She must now battle the prejudices of her family, friends, and church and come to peace with her new sexuality before she can hope to win the affections of the woman of her dreams. But will love be enough?

~ Because a publisher should stand behind their authors~

When Delaney Delacroix is called to locate a missing girl, she never plans on getting caught up with a human trafficking investigation or with the local witch. Meeting with Raelin Montrose changes her life in so many ways that Delaney isn't sure that this isn't destiny.

Raelin Montrose is a practicing Wiccan, and when the ley lines that run under her home tell her that someone is coming, she can't imagine that she was going to solve a mystery and find the love of her life at the same time.

www.shadoepublishing.com

~ *Because a publisher should stand behind their authors~*

Carrie flees from the demons of her present, trying to protect the ones she loves.

Frankie hides from the demons of her past, and the memory of loved ones she failed to protect.

A modern day princess thrown to the wolves, Carrie's only hope is the rancher who had spent the better part of a decade in self imposed, near total, isolation. Frankie's history of losing those she tries to save haunts her, but this madman threatens her home, her livestock, her sanctuary. She knows she can't do it alone, has she still got enough support from her oldest friends?

www.shadoepublishing.com

~ Because a publisher should stand behind their authors~

Amelia Gittens had the credit of being the first and only woman thus far in the United States military of being a sniper in combat, made possible by being in the Military Police unit of the crack 10th Mountain Infantry Division. After retirement she joins the City of New York Police Department, and suddenly finds herself involved in a suspect shooting incident which soon encroaches upon her entire life. In order to protect her therapist who has been targeted as a revenge killing, Amelia takes on the responsibility as if she was still in the Army, treating it as a tactical maneuver.

www.shadoepublishing.com

~ Because a publisher should stand behind their authors~

When U.S. Marine Dakota McKnight returned home from her third tour in Operation Iraqi Freedom, she carried more baggage than the gear and dress blues she had deployed with. A vicious rocket-propelled grenade attack on her base left her best friend dead and Dakota physically and emotionally wounded. The marine who once carried herself with purpose and confidence, has returned broken and haunted by the horrors of war. When she returns to the civilian world, life is not easy, but with the help of her therapist, Janie, she is barely managing to hold her life together...then she meets Beth.

Beth Kendrick is an American history college professor. She is as straight-laced as they come, until Dakota enters her life, that is. Will her children understand what she is going through? Will she take a chance on the broken marine or decide to wait for the perfect someone to come along?

Time is on your side, they say, unless there is a dark, sinister evil at work. Is their love strong enough to hold these two people together? Will the love of a good woman help Dakota find the path to recovery? Or is she doomed to a life of inner turmoil and destruction that knows no end?

www.shadoepublishing.com

*If you have enjoyed this book and the others listed here
Shadoe Publishing, LLC is always looking for first, second, or
third time authors. Please check out our website @
www.shadoepublishing.com
For information or to contact us @
shadoepublishing@gmail.com.*

*We may be able to help you bring your dreams of becoming a
published author to life.*